Short Stories

Anton Z. Capri

Copyright © 2012 Author Name

All rights reserved.

ISBN:1530476356
ISBN-13:9781530476350

DEDICATION

To all of you, who have read my stories and thought, or at least told me that you thought, that they were worth putting in print in front of the world, I thank you and dedicate these stories to you. I hope the rest of the world agrees with you

CONTENTS

	Acknowledgments	i
1	Adonis and Aphrodite	1
2	Minky the Cat	8
3	Unforgiving	12
4	The Expert	30
5	The Stoic	40
6	Misfortune and Fortune	48
7	That's Life	57
8	Authority	67
9	Coming to Canada	73
10	The Burglar-Proof Door	77
11	Dream Buck	88
12	John's Millions	95
13	The Accident	99
14	Bergisel	103
15	Bowron Lakes	106
16	Communists I Have Known	109
17	Concerts in Innsbruck	117
18	Grandmother	119
19	Romanian Traffic Jam	122
20	Sarah	126
21	Macho Challenge	129
22	Meanook Centennial	135
23	Meeting by Chance	146
24	Liesl	151

25	My First Real Drink	155
26	Opening Day in Italy	157
27	Theology and Pride	160
28	The Condom	165
29	Wojczek	169
30	Virginity	173
31	World Shakers	183
32	What If?	188
33	Train Trip	195
34	Third Choice	205
35	Unexpected Family Connections	209
36	The Proposition	211
37	The Big Tree	213
38	Sledding Too Late	217
39	Saving	219
40	There is More to Life	223
41	Schrödinger's Cat	230
42	Retirement Speech	236

AUTHOR	239

ACKNOWLEDGMENTS

To my dear wife of more than half a century, my heartfelt love and thanks for your support and patience while I indulged my passion for writing. You have always been the most important thing in my life. Thank you!

— 1 —
Adonis and Aphrodite

By the time I was born in 2216, the western world had solved its two most salient problems: the population explosion and unemployment due to machines taking over from humans. It was actually the serendipitous solution of the first problem that led to the solution of the second.

It all started, as I heard it told, by a bunch of nerds in Toronto coming up with the idea to improve the Fifi series of robots designed to serve as maids. The nerds developed a wholly new series — the Aphrodites . These were designed as voluptuous models that would not only work as maids, but as willing and fully functional mistresses (lovers if you wish) of young man. These models were so successful that soon many young women lost their beaux and clamored for a male version designed as a lover for women. The nerds went at it again and came up with the Adonis series.

There was a loud outcry from the various religious leaders, especially as the marriage rate and birthrate of children dropped dramatically. What beautiful woman would settle for a mere untalented human lover when she could have an Adonis versed and skilled in all the arts of lovemaking without any of the commitments and risks of becoming pregnant? For a while men too were upset because women ignored them, but the lure of a sexy female robot that was always available, made no demands; and could cook and clean house at the same time was just too alluring. The men settled down.

It was during this period of male discontent that, in order to increase sales, the nerds again improved the Aphrodite model. A man could now choose between the standard models or go for the deluxe series. The deluxe series meant that the customer had to allow various parts of his body hooked up to a device like a lie detector. He was then shown short video clips of seductive women. His involuntary responses showed which of these most stimulated his subconscious mind. That way he always got, not exactly what he thought he wanted, but what he really wanted in a love robot.

Since I had the wherewithal, I bought a deluxe model and named her Desirée. She was everything I could want in a woman without the bother of having to please her. Desirée was there to please me. Her house cleaning was all I could wish for; her cooking was of the finest gourmet type. Her lovemaking was athletic and varied; she knew how to give me pleasure. Whether it was the way she rotated her hips, or contracted in a vigorous climax just as I came, she seemed to sense what gave me the most physical pleasure and then do it. I could not imagine ever wanting to exchange Desirée for a real woman. What could one of these self-centered, difficult to understand; real women ever do for me that Desirée could not?

If it had not been for Gerry, I could have gone on like this for the rest of my life. He spoiled it. Gerry and I met every weekday for lunch at the Club. He was married to Janet — had been for at least fifteen years. His curiosity about Desirée surfaced during every lunchtime. Finally I asked, "Have you never wanted to have sex with a beautiful robot versed in all the techniques of sex?"

Gerry leaned back in his chair. "What man has not? When I see one of these gorgeous females — you can't tell if they're machines — I wonder what it would be like to have those ripe breasts under me as I push inside her, but then I realize that's not real. Even if she were a real human, she would not know my little failings; my flaws and I would be uncomfortable. Janet knows my flaws. There's a real comfort in that."

"What do you mean there's a comfort in Janet knowing your flaws?"

Gerry stared at his apple pie for a while before he answered. "When you have sex with Desirée you have no reason to try to please her. She's there simply to attend to your physical body. That's not what lovemaking is like for me. My biggest turn-on is if I can get Janet deeply aroused, if I can see the change in her eyes, if I can feel her hips thrust up against me, if I can feel the spasms deep inside her as she comes. For me that's a real union of two spirits. It's not just simple rutting. Do you understand?"

I didn't quite understand, but ignored his question. "When I have sex with Desirée, I can feel her climax, her hips thrust up against me. I have all that. So, what's the difference? "

Gerry shook his head almost sadly. "You poor man, you don't understand. Your Desirée will have these automatic responses no matter what you do. That's how she's programmed. She'll have this mechanical climax response because that's what her program requires when her sensors say that you're close to climax. You don't have to please her. It's all purely mechanical. There's no union of two spirits like in what I'm talking about."

"Fine, so I don't understand. Explain it to me."

Gerry sat up straighter. "I have no objection to having sex as a purely physical experience, sometimes I do that with Janet, but that is not the same thing as making love. When Janet and I make love, I get my biggest satisfaction out of giving her pleasure, just as I am convinced that giving me pleasure gives her satisfaction. This is not something you can have with a machine. It's not like sticking your cock into a milking machine. There is no reason for you to try to please Desirée because she does not experience physical pleasure. You are simply having sex with her. You don't make love to her. Now, is it clear?"

I'd never thought of it in those terms. So far I'd been very happy to have the physical pleasure, after all that's what men got when they went to a whore. But this was no whore. Desirée was mine. Then why were we men so obsessed with the idea that no other man should have sex with our woman? Gerry seemed to have the answer: we want to be the one that gives her the most pleasure.

Here was something that was missing from my rolls in the hay with Desirée. It wouldn't matter what I did, she would always respond as if this were the best ever. That conversation with Gerry changed my relationship with Desirée. While having sex with her I started to ask her if she liked it, or what I could do to give her more pleasure.

She always gave me one of her bright smiles. "Don't be silly, of course I like it and don't change anything. I like what you're doing."

This went on for some time until one day at work Anita brushed past me on the way to her cubicle. She was an ordinary woman in her late twenties with blue eyes who always wore her blonde hair in long braids that she wrapped across the top of her head — attractive, but not seductive. This time her hair was loose over her shoulders. As she passed me, she apologized for her loose hair, "I was at the gym and didn't have time to do it up. "

I stared after her. The hair made a big difference. She was still not beautiful, but she drew my attention. A few days later, against all my instincts, I asked Anita if I could buy her a drink after work.

"But you have an Aphrodite, a love robot," she replied. "Won't your robot mind?"

I'd never thought of that. "Why should the robot that keeps house for me mind?" I asked.

Her hand shot to her mouth, "Oh, I didn't meant to offend!"

"No offence taken. Now, may I invite you for a drink?"

A smile lit up her face. "Yes, I'd love to have a drink with you."

That's how it started. We had that drink and I enjoyed our conversation so much that I asked her out several more times. She agreed and we started to meet regularly after work. We didn't just talk, we discussed. I found that Anita had a mind of her own, a wonderful mind full of thoughts I had never even contemplated, thoughts different from mine, thoughts, which she was willing to stand up for and defend. Sometimes we disagreed very strongly — I would not call it arguing — we just disagreed. She also understood when to tell me to stop, or when to encourage me. It was refreshing to have an exchange of views that did not end up with my views always being accepted. I sometimes wound up contemplating her views for quite a while until I saw the flaws in my arguments and the logic in hers. More and more I looked forward to our dates. Yes, I started to think of our meetings as dates and wondered when we'd get intimate with each other. But I did not want to spoil our friendship with sex. This was very different from being with Desirée. Somehow my athletic romps with Desirée also became less frequent. I neglected my love robot and dreamed more often of going to bed with Anita.

Things might have gone on in this fashion for some time if Anita hadn't slipped on the ice and broken her leg. I now found myself looking after her. This was a totally new experience for me. Every little victory she achieved in her attempt to get back on her feet was also a source of achievement and joy for me. It was not until later that I realized that caring for her is what drew me closer to her and made me fall in love. Yes, love. It is a strange feeling to want to take care of someone. I was beginning to understand what Gerry talked about. Anita was someone I truly cared about, not just someone to have sex with, but someone I wanted to take care of, someone with whom I could share intimate things. I proposed to her and we got married as soon s she was able to walk again.

We've been married now for more than thirty years and I still discover new things about Anita every week. That was not something that ever happened with Desirée. With her it was pure sex, nothing else. With Anita it is a sharing of minds.

What really drew us together was having to struggle. My father disapproved of this marriage and we were cut off from any financial support from him. Our first house needed a lot of renovating. Anita was always there, not just beside me, but with a hammer, and whatever tool was required in her hand, and she was using it. At night when we went to bed we were often too tired for sex, but the sheer joy of holding each other was as good as the best sex. Working together for a common goal is what made our love grow.

Yes, Anita kept Desirée, but only as a maid. Anita is the only one that now interacts with Desirée. That's just fine with me. The lovemaking — not just plain sex — with Anita is not as athletic as with Desirée, but it is more satisfying. Also as I age, sex has assumed less importance in my life. I am content to be able to embrace Anita and know that she is there to support me if I need encouragement or support.

— 2 —

Minky, The Cat

Maureen, my best friend, bought this beautiful Russian blue cat. It cost a fortune, but she thought it was worth it. After meeting Minky, the cat, I am inclined to agree. Shorthaired with silver tipped guard hairs Minky is sleek and beautiful. Every time I visited Maureen, I saw how attached she and Minky had become. This cat with round green eyes and large pointed ears followed Maureen around the house like a shadow. Every so often, Maureen bent down to scratch the cat's head and be rewarded her with a gentle purr. They seemed of one heart and mind. I was almost envious of this sleek feline that had so completely captured my best friend's affection.

I tended to avoid touching the cat and sat further than usual from Maureen so as not have to be in proximity to Minky. Maureen must have noticed, because she asked, "Are you afraid or jealous of Minky?"

"What a silly question! Why do you ask?" I replied.

"It's just that you seem to avoid being close to him."

Several months after the arrival of Minky, Maureen asked me if I could look after her cat for a day while she went to Calgary for a meeting of regional writers. Of course I agreed, but I would need a list of instructions on how to look after Minky. No problem. When Maureen brought Minky to my house, she also brought his scratching post, food, litter box, and a printed list of instructions. I was all set.

The next morning I fed Minky, but he seemed a little shy around me. The instructions said to leave him in the house whenever I left. This suited me fine. I hoped he would eat while I went outside. It was a beautiful day and I wanted to plant some bushes and other perennials.

Two hours later I was sweaty, dirty, and satisfied with my accomplishments as I took off my work shoes to reenter the house. The screen door was not latched; the old spring no longer pulled the door shut. No matter, this was a job for another day when I did not have to look after Minky. Inside the kitchen I noticed that Minky had eaten some of the food in his dish. Good! Now I needed to find him to give him the petting that he expected every morning. I called his name, but he did not come. Of course not, he was shy with everyone except Maureen. I searched through the house: under the living room sofa and chairs, under the beds, everywhere. No cat.

He must have found a really good place to hide. I commenced to search more carefully. Still no cat. I searched again and again, calling, "Minky," with increasing nervousness. After more than five futile searches through my house I realized that the cat was not in the house. How could I have been so careless as to leave the screen door unlatched? The cat must have slipped outside.

Forgotten was my desire for a shower and a soothing cup of tea, after my work outside. I had to fine Maureen's cat. Once outside I again called, "Minky," over and over again. I searched throughout the yard, under the bushes, among the flowers. No cat. By noon I had to admit that Minky was lost. How was I going to face Maureen?

Maybe a shower and a cup of tea would help me to think of what to do. The shower and tea did not help. I phoned the SPCA and told them that I had lost this beautiful Russian blue cat. Would they let me know if anyone found. They asked if the cat had a chip. That way they could notify all the veterinarians to check any Russian blue that came in to them. I said I didn't know. They offered little hope. "Russian blues are very expensive and if someone finds the cat, they are unlikely to report it to us," the lady on the phone said.

I could not help thinking of how I failed my best friend and lost her beautiful companion. Would Maureen ever be able to forgive me or would she think I did this on purpose? It would be horrible to lose my best friend over this incident.

I spent a terrible day going over and over in my mind as to why I had not checked whether the screen door was properly latched. That night I could not fall asleep and when I eventually did sleep I had this horrible dream in which Minky's body was found on a road mangled and flattened by car tires. I woke up tired and anxious as I prepared myself to face Maureen.

When Maureen arrived and after our greetings she looked at

me and asked, "What's the matter? You look terrible. Tell me."

"I've lost Minky," I blurted.

Maureen's face changed to one of deep concern. "Tell me how."

So, I told her. She sat in a chair across from me and listened attentively. When I was finished, she arose and walked over to me. I expected her to lash out at me. But no, instead of a tongue-lashing, Maureen put her arms around me and in a warm hug said, "I'm so sorry to have put you into a situation like this. Please forgive me."

"Oh Maureen, it's all my stupid fault. Please forgive me.'

After that we both had a good cry. When Maureen got up to leave she said, "At least let me see what you planted."

Once out in the yard, she gain broke down. "Oh Minky, I miss you so."

She had barely finished speaking when we heard a soft, "Miaow," emanate from under the wooden porch and a bedraggled Minky crawled out.

— 3 —

Unforgiving

After I handed the reins to Michael and climbed off Wind, Michael passed me a glass of cool lemonade. While I sipped the refreshing drink he reached behind the wooden boards of the stall and brought forth a bouquet of wild flowers. Every morning after my ride, Michael performed these little gestures that meant so much to me.

As I strolled from the stables back to our house I admired the high stonewall that surrounded the old maple trees and gave shelter to our property. The leaves in the maples whispered to each other and almost drowned out he rhythmic crash of the waves on the shores of Long Island.

At the door I stopped to think. It was not easy to anticipate Papa's response. How would he react if I told him? He's very old-fashioned and class conscious even though we are already into the twentieth century. Maybe it's good that I've kept my talks with Michael secret. Even Mama, were she still alive, would not understand. I can just hear her, "How could you even think of associating with a servant boy whose job it is to make sure the stables are clean and the horses are curried? It just isn't done. Get it out of your mind."

To me it doesn't matter that Michael is just a stable hand; he's also different, not at all like the boys Papa favors and encourages me to associate with. He's serious and kind and thoughtful.

The few conversations we've had showed me that he has serious thoughts and ambitions. He doesn't want to be a stable boy all his life; he wants to become expert with horses: a successful horse trainer. Maybe it would be better if I kept my thoughts about him secret for a little longer, at least until I've talked more with him and we have an understanding and I've prepared Papa.

I continued riding every day and as my conversations with Michael grew longer I looked forward to them. He knew so much about horses, almost as much as Maestro Palucci knew about singing and opera. To me, riding on Wind was almost as exciting as my singing and piano lessons, where the maestro kept repeating what a wonderful voice I have, that with more training I could be a professional opera singer. I wanted to believe him, but knew that this was not part of my destiny. According to Papa, I was destined to be the wife of the successful son of one of his colleagues.

From Palucci I learned about breath and voice control; from Michael I learned about dressage. Along with opera I took to studying the books about horses and horse training in Papa's library. With Michael's guidance I practiced my newly acquired knowledge on Wind, who promised to be a good jumper.

My problems, or should I say good fortune, started after a most successful ride on Wind. I was preparing for the horse show. Wind cleared the circuit in record time without a single fault. I was so thrilled that when I jumped off, instead of throwing Michael the reins, I threw my arms around him. At that moment, Papa happened by. He didn't say a word, just continued walking. I released Michael, with a premonition of something serious, and stared after Papa's departing back.

The next day when I went to the stable, Wind was not saddled and ready. He was gone. I looked for Michael to get an explanation. He also was gone. I rushed back into the house, to Papa's study. "What happened to Michael and Wind?"

Papa looked up from his desk. "Good morning, Tamara," he said in even tones as his deep-set eyes bored into me. "That is no way for a seventeen year old daughter to greet her father. Good morning. Now go outside, and come back in, and do it right."

I returned his glare, and did something I didn't realize I could. I stamped my foot and shouted, "No! What happened to Michael and Wind? They're not in the stable."

Papa's eyes never left my face. Although my knees were starting to wobble, and I felt spiders crawling over my belly, I stared back without blinking. We glared at each other for more than a minute before he said, "Leave my office and don't come back until you know how to behave." His gaze returned to his desktop.

"You fired Michael and sold Wind, didn't you? Why?"

Papa looked up. "Because you didn't know how to behave and needed a lesson."

I didn't believe that Papa could be that unfeeling. He knew that I loved Wind — had trained him to be a jumper — and that I definitely wasn't interested in any of those pea cocky sons of his friends. "But Wind was my horse. I taught him. You had no right to sell him. And what about Michael?"

"No, Wind was my property and I had every right to sell him. As for that stable boy, no daughter of mine is going to throw herself at such a creature. He had to go."

"Michael's not a creature. He's a human just like you and I."

Papa looked at me as if in shock. He spoke in a soft voice. "No, my daughter, not like you and I. He isn't and couldn't ever be in the same class as the daughter of Reginald Belsingham. He was born into his class and that's where he belongs. He was aiming at something unattainable when he embraced you."

"But he didn't embrace me. I embraced him."

"All the worse. It means that things had already gone too far. He had to go."

"In that case I also have to go." I regretted my statement as soon as I'd uttered it. I knew I'd gone too far, but could not back down now. Something terrible had passed. Papa's eyes again pierced me. In the silence that now cloaked the room like a dark shroud, I heard the clock ticking behind him. Despite the feeling that I'd gone too far, I refused to lower my eyes.

After another interminable time, Papa sighed and said, "That choice is yours, but realize this. If you leave this house without my blessing, I will no longer have a daughter. Now leave my office and decide what you want to do."

I turned without a word and closed the door softly and went to my room where I packed a few garments and my jewelry. I was too angry to think. I had no idea where to go, but go I must. The idea of being on my own both frightened and excited me.

Sure I'd miss my room. But then, on the plus side, I would not have to cater to Papa's dictatorial moods and ideas. I knew that he did not understand that I was a modern woman. Women were now able to vote in the State of New York. This was 1917. Hadn't Jeanette Rankin of Montana become the first woman to be elected to the U.S. House of Representatives? She had, and I, Tamara Belsingham, would also join these pioneers in freeing women from the chains imposed by dictatorial men like Papa.

* * *

It was still morning, not even light yet, when three weeks later, I stumbled past the gate, up the tree lined, curved path to the door and rang the bell of my father's house. My adventure in becoming a fighter for women's freedom had not turned out the way I'd hoped. I'd not known how to husband the money from my jewels. The first shop that advertised, "We buy and sell old jewelry," bought all my jewels for whatever the owner offered. Also, I ate at expensive restaurants. When the money got scarce, I became a bit more frugal and took lodgings in a boarding house instead of the Waldorf where I used to stay with my father when I accompanied him to Manhattan.

My money ran out three days ago and having nowhere to turn, much as I resisted the idea, I felt forced to return home to my father and submit to his will. It took all my willpower and remaining strength to hike the miles out to Long Island, to my father's estate. I hadn't eaten for three days and realized that I could not go on without food. My vision was unclear — all I looked at was foggy as if seen through a cheese cloth. I'd reached the end of my endurance. It was this realization that brought me back to face my father's will.

William, the butler, opened the door and, losing his usual composure, gasped. "Miss Tamara."

Before he could utter another word, father arrived to ask, "Who is it?"

"Miss Tamara, your daughter, Sir," William said.

I heard father say, "Close the door, William. I have no daughter."

That was it. If he thought I was going to beg he was wrong. I swayed as I stared at the closed door. Father had rejected me. He would not take me back or even ask if I needed help.

As I stumbled down the curved path to the road, I vowed that never again would he have the opportunity to do this to me. I'd rather die than give him the satisfaction to tell me that he was right. He'd be sorry when they found my emaciated body outside his estate. When he had to look at my corpse. Yes, he'd be sorry.

I fought my body's weakness and reached the gate. Before I passed through the large gate, a beam of light from the open door of the mansion reached me, but I did not look back to see who'd opened the door. Was it William, or my father? I don't know

Outside the gate I crumpled against the stonewall that surrounded the mansion. Too stunned, exhausted, and angry to cry I rested, trying to gather strength to continue — but where. I'd reached my end.

I must have fainted because the next thing I remember is that someone was shaking my shoulder and a man's voice said, "Miss, Miss, are you all right?"

"Yes, just hungry."

Arms pulled me to my feet and the same voice said, "Can you stand?"

I managed to croak, "Yes."

With the man's arms helping me, I arose. "Good, now come along, we'll get you something to eat. I'm heading to Greenwich Village."

The man helped me into a hansom and we headed toward New York City. On the way he introduced himself as Clarence Slim.

Without thinking, I extended my hand and answered, "Pleased to meet you. I'm Tamara Belsingham." His hand felt like a dead fish.

"How do you do, Miss Belsingham," he said. "A relative of the wealthy Mr. Reginald Belsingham, where I picked you up?"

This was too funny. I emitted a weak laugh. "Would I be here with you if I were?"

"No, of course not."

As we rode on, I stole glances at the man sitting across from me. He seemed to be examining me closely. I didn't know why, but the way he stared at me was unpleasant. He appeared to be in his late thirties. His clothing was neat, but lacked elegance and taste: a scarlet ascot crowded like an oversized goiter between the huge lapels of his jacket; his large watery eyes bulged below straight thin brows. A narrow black mustache carved a sharp line above broad, sensuous lips. Not at all someone I would have trusted if I hadn't been that desperate.

* * *

Once in Greenwich Village, we stopped in front of a modest inn where, after paying for the cab, Mr. Slim led me into the dining room. He ordered meals for both of us and, while I ate, he leaned back to study me more carefully. "You're no servant girl, are you?" It was more of a statement than a question.

"Why do you say that?"

"You neither eat, nor speak like one. Your manners are those of a lady, someone born to the upper classes, to wealth. Are you perhaps the bastard daughter or even a mistress of Mr. Belsingham?"

This shocked me and I paused with the fork partway to my mouth. "How dare you?"

"I just wondered about finding you in front of his estate and having the same last name."

"I am neither and even though you are feeding me, I do not wish to be insulted."

"When did you last eat?" the man asked.

I swallowed before answering, "Three days ago."

The man nodded as if in agreement. "A long time between meals. Do you want to tell me what happened?"

"I think not. I am grateful for your help Mr. Slim, but you and I are strangers and this story is personal."

He extended his hand, pale with thin blue veins. "Call me Slim."

"Miss Tamara Belsingham."

"Well, Miss Belsingham," Slim said. "I'll ask again. Perhaps you're a distant relative of the wealthy Mr. Reginald Belsingham, where I picked you up?"

Tamara laughed. "As I said before, would I be here with you in this place if I were?"

He nodded with a knowing leer. "Of course not. By the way, have you made plans for your lodgings for tonight? Where do you plan to sleep?"

With food in me, I felt stronger. I ate the rest of the greasy mutton while considering how to answer this inquisitive Mr. Slim. "It's not even noon yet. I have still time to make plans. I'll find some place."

"How would you like to later have dinner with me and spend the night in this inn?"

I regarded him with what I hoped was a stern, reprimanding look of shock. "Why Mr. Slim, what a bold proposal. I may be starving, but even so, I do consider myself a lady."

"As I said, call me Slim, not Mr. Slim. And I'm sorry if I offended you. I only want to be of assistance."

"And why would you want to be of assistance to someone you've just met?"

"You're in need of help and I'm a Christian."

Slim's face displayed no signs of irony. He maintained a placid mask that hid any chance of reading his thoughts or feelings. Even though I knew that it was unladylike to accept his offer, I had little alternative.

A week earlier, when I'd managed to find Michael at one of the stables, he'd pointed out to me that he never entertained any of the ideas that I'd believed he harbored or wanted him to have. In fact, he was angry and annoyed with me for getting him sacked and he viewed my entire predicament as ridiculous. After all, I was the rich daughter of Mr. Belsingham. How could I possibly be short of money?

By now I was painfully aware that it hadn't taken long for me to spend the money I got from selling my jewelry and extra clothing and that I no longer had any money left to buy food or shelter. I also realized that I was unequipped to earn my keep. So, my reputation might be tarnished if I accepted Mr. Slim's proposal, but then my prospects without a dowry or inheritance had also already vanished. There was little more I could lose. Besides in all the novels I'd read there was always the gentlemanly, kind stranger who came to the aid of ladies in distress.

Attempting a friendly smile I said, "I accept your most Christian offer, Slim. And once I'm able, I shall repay you."

Slim smiled showing his teeth. It reminded me of a predator about to pounce. "I'm sure you will. In that case I'll book the room now," he said.

The rest of the day as we strolled about the streets of Manhattan, only stopping for lunch, Slim accompanied me. His constant surveillance made me nervous. By evening we were back at the inn and Slim ordered a large meal along with wine and grog. As I ate, he encouraged me to taste the grog. When I declined, he poured wine for me, surreptitiously refilling my glass when he thought I wasn't looking. I didn't want to admit that I'd never tasted wine. It tasted like sour lemonade. By the time the meal was over, I felt light headed and unsteady on my feet.

Slim took my arm and guided me up the stairs to a room. It lacked any of the amenities and grace of my bedroom at home. A white bowl on a rickety table between a white ewer filled with water and a massive pewter candleholder without a candle was meant to serve as a means for one's ablutions. A threadbare towel rested beside the bowl. On the other side of the table a bed covered by a gray blanket stood out from the wall. I glanced around this Spartan room and asked, "Is this my bedroom?"

"Our bedroom," Slim answered as he reached behind him, locked the door, removed the key, and placed it in his pocket.

"But where are you going to sleep? There's only one bed." I said.

"We will share the bed."

Now I understood. Slim was a cad. My right hand flew to my mouth. "No, I can't. I must leave."

Slim grabbed my arm and tossed me on the bed. "I told you I'm a Christian and I'd help you. I can't allow you to go out on the streets by yourself at night and I can't afford a separate room for you. Now get undressed and get into bed." He started to remove his jacket and untie the scarlet ascot.

My mind was racing, searching for an idea of how to escape from this predicament. I had no money, no valuables, but I still had my pride and, I was in no doubt that this man meant to ravish me. I had to find a way to distract him. Arising from the bed I undid my blouse.

"That's better," said Slim watching me with wet lips and shining eyes.

After removing the blouse, I wandered over to the bowl and filled it with water.

"What're you doing?" Slim asked.

"My evening ablutions."

"Go ahead," he said.

As he pulled his shirt over his head I acted, without thinking, seized the pewter candleholder and smashed him on the head. His knees buckled and he crumpled to the floor. Feelings of relief and anxiety conflicted in my mind as I bent over him. I've killed him, I thought. His chest rose and fell. He was still breathing.

I breathed a sigh of relief. He's still alive. Thank God. I have to get out of here before he awakes. But I need the key. I re-buttoned my blouse and reached down to search Slim's pockets for the door key. My hand lit upon the key and his wallet. When I pulled the wallet out, I found that it was stuffed with bills of various denominations. After a moment's hesitation I extracted three twenty dollar bills from the wallet, placed it back in his pocket and let myself out of the room with the key. I locked the door from the outside and left the key in the lock. Careful that nobody would see me, I stole down the stairs and out of the inn.

A few blocks from the inn I hired a hackney and asked the driver to take me to the railroad station. By now I had evolved a plan. After the cab left, I flagged another cab and asked to be taken to Greenwich Village. There I alit and wandered beneath the now blazing gaslights till I found the boarding house with a sign stating, BOARDING HOUSE FOR RESPECTABLE YOUNG LADIES. This was where I'd stayed before my money ran out.

The owner, a grim-faced woman in her early fifties, viewed me with suspicion. "It's a little late to be looking for a room," she said. " I don't tolerate prostitutes"

The insinuation hurt. I wanted to turn around and leave, but didn't know where else to go. I said, "In spite of the late hour, I'm not a loose woman. But please, you know me. I stayed here before. I'm in need of a place to stay and I can pay in advance."

I didn't know whether it was the offer of payment in advance that convinced the owner to rent me a room. After I was shown to the tiny room, I was grateful, in spite of its size, to get it for twenty dollars a week including meals.

The next morning I started looking for a job. I didn't know what I'd be able to do, but knew I had to find work. I was never going back to Father and I knew that the money I'd taken from Slim would not last. As I strolled north, in the direction of Manhattan, I passed a nightclub with a sign: SINGER WANTED.

Inside the dim establishment chairs were piled upside down on the tables in the middle of the room. In one corner a young man looked up from a table where he was reading by the light of a candle and asked, "May I help you?"

"I'm a singer, looking for a job."

"What can you sing?"

"Opera."

The man looked me up and down. "Opera! Really?"

"Yes, really." I answered with as much assurance as I could muster. His detailed examination of my attire unsettled me. My dress was almost certainly wrinkled and I had not been able to adjust my coiffure without the help of a maid. I was ready to bolt.

"I'd give you an audition, but here's no one to play the accompaniment," he said.

"I can play the accompaniment myself, if you have a piano," I said.

The man stood up and pointed to a piano off in the corner of a tiny stage and said, "Show me."

I walked over to the piano, struck a few chords and, after a few deep breaths, broke into the most demanding aria I knew: *Der Hölle Rache* (Hell's Revenge) from Mozart's The Magic Flute. I wanted to impress him with my ability. The dimly lit room seemed to brighten as I lost myself in the music. I felt my voice and the piano accompaniment fill the room as if an entire orchestra were playing. The man wandered closer to the stage. He sank down into a chair to listen.

When I finished, he stood and applauded. "Bravo, that's magnificent. You belong in an opera, not in a cabaret."

I curtsied and said, "Thank you, but I need a job, not a compliment." His voice was pleasant. I now took a closer look at him. He was maybe five to ten years older than I. His attire was elegant and neat. He was clean-shaven. Brown hair was combed straight back from a high brow. Altogether a friendly face

"I can find you a job, but on one condition," he said.

I found the hair on my nape bristling. "What's the condition?"

"I become your agent and if I get you a part in an opera, even only a minor part, you will accept."

I was skeptical. "What exactly does an agent do? And what

would I have to do for you?"

The man regarded me more closely. "You mean to say with a voice like that you've never had an agent?"

"No, I haven't, but you haven't answered my question."

"An agent is someone who handles your business affairs. He gets bookings for you, and tries to further your career. For this you pay the agent a percentage of your earning. I'll settle for ten per cent."

"Ten per cent!"

"Yes, ten per cent." His voice was firm. "But you still need voice lessons and you'll have to pay for that yourself. In the meantime I'll get you a job in this cabaret, playing the piano."

I was pleased and astonished. "What about singing?" I asked. "I thought you needed a singer."

"I don't need a singer. This cabaret does. Singing here would not be good for your voice. Cabaret singing requires a different style from opera. If you do one, you won't be able to do the other. Well, is it a deal?"

I studied this handsome man extending his hand to me. Could I trust him?

* * *

The scenery flashed by outside the window of the Pullman as the train hurtled east. I stared out and marveled at the magic of the last twenty years. Europe was now preparing for all out war with that insane monster with the ridiculous mustache. The USA had suffered during the depression, many fortunes were wiped out, but I had prospered thanks to James Calhoun, my agent and husband.

The maniac that ruled Germany had just invaded Poland. Manufacturing was again in full swing, and the USA was recovering.

After the first three years in New York, during which time James made me work long hours at my music lessons, interrupted only by my piano playing at the cabaret, he had finally declared me ready. We then travelled to San Francisco where, after several minor roles, James landed me, a chance as an understudy as Olympia, the mechanical doll, in Offenbach's Tales of Hoffmann. I never expected to be called to perform, but I was, and when Gaetano Merola recognized my talent, my career was launched. Now, after so many years, I was returning to New York to the Metropolitan Opera as a diva to perform as Ciocio-san in Madame Butterfly. Even though at just under forty I was entering the last stages of an almost magical career, life could not be better.

* * *

Although drained of energy from my performance and drunk with applause, adulation, and champagne, I marveled at how wonderful life was. After this smashing success as Ciocio-san at the Met, life could not get better. When James entered my dressing room, I turned to greet him with a smile.

"There's a man, calling himself Reginald Belsingham and claiming to be your father just outside the door, asking to see you," he said.

"What does he want?" I asked.

"He didn't say."

"Open the door and let me have a look at him."

James walked to the door and opened it. I turned in my chair and saw just outside the door a stooped, with head down, shabby, and aged caricature of the once dapper Reginald Belsingham. For a brief moment I wanted to get up and embrace the frail husk that remained of my one-time excessively proud father. The tenderness in my heart, at the thought that his harshness had led to my success, turned to steel as I recalled the last words I'd hear him speak. Momentarily I again became Ciocio-san rejected by Mr. Pinkerton and robbed of her child, but unlike that heroic woman I did not contemplate suicide. No! Life had tempered me into sterner stuff. I turned my back to the door and said to James, "Please tell Mr. Belsingham that, as I recall, he once stated that he has no daughter."

— 4 —

The Expert

When Kimberly Clarke hired me straight out of university to work in their Pioneering Research Department, I was more than happy. My degree in Engineering Physics would actually come to good use. I'd worked for Kimberly Clarke the previous summer and had found out about their Pioneering Research department. In my mind it was an elite department devoted entirely to solving problems that were more fundamental than what one would expect to encounter in a pulp and paper company — exactly what I wanted. That department was small: three physicists, one biologist and one chemist, three technicians, as well as another chemist who was the director. All of them, except for me, had a Ph. D. I would be working with brilliant people and have a chance to learn a lot from them.

My first project was a big success and even got a patent. I was on my way to become what I had always wanted — a research scientist. Life was good. Then, one morning, the director, John Casey, came to me and said, "Tony, It's your turn to go to a mill. At the converting mill in Iron Mountain they have a problem with hard wrinkles and you have to go there as an expert to solve this."

I stared at John with my mouth hanging open until I recovered myself. "But I've never been in a converting mill. I don't have a clue what hard wrinkles are."

He smiled, "That's not the point. You're from Pioneering Research. That's supposed to make you smarter than the average bear, at least in the minds of the people who work in the mills. That's why you're going. Oh, and before you go, you should see Ralph Kruger in the Engineering department. He's about to retire and he'll tell you all you need to know."

"So, why not send him?"

"He's about to retire, and not from Pioneering Research. You are. That makes you an expert."

That was the end of the conversation and that's how I wound up in the conversion mill at Iron Mountain. But first I visited Ralph Kruger.

* * *

"So, it's hard wrinkles they've got?" Ralph asked.

I nodded and asked, "What are hard wrinkles?"

Ralph looked me up and down. "You're pretty green, aren't you? Right out of college?"

I nodded.

"In that case we'd better get you educated." He went over to a shelf and pulled out a large binder. When he opened it, I saw a photograph of a machine that made the man standing near it look like an ant. "That's a paper machine," Ralph said. "It's about as long as a large city block, and fifteen feet wide. The sheet on those reels travels at about 1, 500 feet a minute. He flipped a couple of pages and showed a giant reel wrapped in a huge roll of paper. "That's the take-up reel. Now for your hard wrinkles." He flipped back a few pages to a photograph of a sheet between two reels. "Those are calender reels. They iron or calender the coating on the paper so that it is entirely smooth and shiny. You got that?"

I nodded, mutely. I wasn't sure I understood it all, but I realized that the paper machine displayed in these photographs was a giant beast and I would be expected to tame it.

"This is where the hard wrinkles occur," Ralph pointed at the calender reels. "If the sheet going between these reels isn't completely flat, a small fold occurs and when that fold is calendered, it produces what we call a hard wrinkle. Hard wrinkles are bad, because the paper is cut by these wrinkles and the publisher who buys our product has to discard that paper. Of course we catch these mistakes before they get to our customers." Ralph stopped and looked at me with a satisfied look.

I returned his gaze and asked, "So, how do you fix hard wrinkles?"

"You don't. You make sure that they don't happen in the first place." Again he looked at me with that superior smile.

"O.K. How do you prevent hard wrinkles?"

"Now you asked the right question. That's why we have something called a Beloit Reel. That's a reel made out of several sections so that it can have a 'Wow' in it. In other words, it's curved, but only a little bit, not so you can see the curve. The idea is for the curve to spread the sheet. But, to work, the curve has to point into the sheet. There's an arrow on the end of the reel that shows which way the curve points. That arrow has to point into the sheet." Again he cast that questioning and admonishing look at me. I opened my mouth, but he held up his hand and said, "My advice to you is for you to get to know the machine tender — that's the guy sitting on a high chair like a life guard watching the machine — he'll know what's wrong."

* * *

Iron Mountain had a very nice hotel with a good restaurant and bar. The paper mill was the only industry in this town. Since I was on a company expense account, I had a great room and enjoyed my meal after I arrived. The next morning I marched over to the mill, introduced myself to the manager who got me a visitor's tag, and took me to meet Gordon, the plant engineer, a man in his mid forties. The manager told him to give me all the help I needed and left. After the manager left, Gordon looking anything but friendly turned to me, "Well, Tony, we don't need any help from you bright guys from Pioneering Research. We can solve our own problems, but go ahead and look around. I'm curious to see what an expert like you'll find." He turned and walked away, leaving me standing inside his glass-walled office.

I walked out into the moisture laden, noisy plant, where the air carried a hint of yeast. Later I learned that this was due to the clay used as part of the coating on high quality paper. In front of me stretched the giant machine with the sheet of paper rushing by at tremendous speed. Affecting the air of someone long accustomed to working in a paper mill I strolled the length of the machine to the end, to the take up reel.

A man controlling an electric winch was bout to remove the full reel and replace it with a steel core. He first lowered the steel core into its cradle where it started to rotate. When the paper reached the empty reel, he neatly sliced the fifteen-foot wide sheet with a high-pressure air hose and, using the air from the hose as an extension of his arm, wrapped the sheet on the empty reel. He then lifted the full reel out of its cradle onto a forklift.

I approached the driver of the forklift. "Hi, how's it going? I'm Tony."

"I'm Jack," he shouted back. He reached to change gears.

"How we doing for hard wrinkles?" I asked.

He stepped out of the forklift and walked around to the front where he pointed at an ugly fold in the middle of the reel. "Look for yourself. You're from Pioneering Research, ain't you?"

"Yes, I am. How long's this been happening?"

"Four days."

"Where you taking this reel?"

"To the warehouse. We can get two six-foot reels out of it. The damaged middle portion will have to be repulped."

"Pretty costly business."

"Yeah." He climbed back on his forklift and drove away.

I strolled back to where the machine tender sat in his elevated chair. Ralph Kruger had told me, "As long as the machine tender is sitting on his ass, the company's making money." Clearly the company was making money. I looked up at a man in his early fifties. His belly bulged over his knees and accented the size of the man. He must have been at least six feet four and three hundred pounds. He smiled down at me.

"Hi," I said. "I'm Tony. How's it going?"

"I know who you are. You're the guy from Pioneering Research. I'm Sven, Sven Peterson."

"You're right, Sven that's who I am. What time do you get off?"

"I just started. I'll be off at six. Why?"

"Well, if you have time, I'd like to buy you a couple of beers."

Sven beamed. "I always have time if someone else is buying."

"All right, Sven. I'll meet you here just before six."

* * *

Sven, as it turned out had the huge capacity for beer that his belly promised. By the time I finished my first pint, he was already on his fourth. I also learned that he wasn't married so I offered to buy him dinner. He accepted without hesitation and ordered the biggest steak the restaurant had to offer.

After the dinner when he leaned back I asked, "So, what's with the hard wrinkles?"

"Oh that. It's the stupid engineer. He's going through a divorce and can't think straight. It's the bloody Beloit reel. It's pointing the wrong way. That's what's causing the problem."

"Can you show me?"

"Nope. That's the plant engineer's department and he'd have my balls in a sling. Besides, a machine tender can't tell nothing to an engineer."

"But you're sure it's the Beloit reel?"

"What else could it be?"

I nodded. "You're right. It couldn't be anything else."

* * *

The next morning I walked into the plant engineer's office. He looked as if he hadn't slept in a week. I hesitated a moment before I said, "Morning, Gordon. Can I buy you a coffee?"

"No thanks."

I started to feel sorry for him. If I felt like he looked, I'd want to curl up in a fetal position and hide from the world. But I had to get through to him. "I need to look at the Beloit reel and since that's your department, I need to go there with you." I didn't want to tell him that I had no idea where this Beloit reel was to be found.

He looked at me through bleary eyes. "We never touch the Beloit reel."

"I know," I said. "But I need to see that it isn't damaged."

"It's not damaged."

I had to find out where the Beloit real was. "I believe you, but I have to check this myself and I can't go there without you. So, are you going to help me or not?"

That last question must have done it because he said, "I know it's a waste of time, but lets go."

The Beloit reel, about eight inches in diameter, rotated above us at high speed as we crouched in the concrete pit below the huge machine. Gordon pointed at the cylinder and sneered, "See it's running the way it's supposed to."

I didn't answer, but ambled over to the end of the reel to look at the arrow that would indicate the direction of the bow. Sure enough, it was pointing in the wrong direction. I returned to Gordon and asked, "Do you mind if I come down here again to watch the reel, to see if anything changes?"

"Suit yourself. Now let's get out of here."

Since I was on an expense account, I continued to buy Sven beer after work for the next two days while I occasionally made my way into the pit below the Beloit reel. Sven became most garrulous after several beers and filled me in on the plant gossip: who was having an affair with whom, where the best fishing streams were in the area, and who was the best fisherman — after Sven, of course.

On the third day, I again approached Gordon. "I know the cause of the hard wrinkles. It's the Beloit reel."

"What's wrong with it?" he snarled.

"It's pointing in the wrong direction. We need to change that."

"We never touch the Beloit reel."

I looked at his face, which with the blood had drained from

his cheeks gave them a sickly pallor. He was the plant engineer and I didn't want to embarrass him, but I had to get that reel rotated. "Look," I said. "I'll take responsibility and even admit that you strongly advised against it. How's that?"

"I don't know. We never touch that reel."

I played my final card. "In that case I'll have to get the plant manager to OK the change."

Gordon looked ready to have a coronary or at least pop a blood vessel. "Fine, but it's on your head. I'll get a machinist and we'll go change the reel setting."

Fifteen minutes later, with a machinist carrying a large wrench in tow, we headed past Sven to the pit under the Beloit reel. Sven winked at me and I winked back. Once at the reel the machinist asked, "Which way d'you want me to rotate the reel?"

I indicated the direction and said, "Go ahead."

The machinist had barely put his wrench to a giant nut at the end of the reel and turned a couple of degrees when Gordon yelled, "Stop, that's enough!"

I looked at the arrow on the end of the reel. It had moved in the right direction, but not enough. "You need to turn it another quarter turn," I said.

"You crazy?" Gordon asked. "You shouldn't turn it at all."

I turned to the machinist and said, "Turn it another forty five degrees. I'll take full responsibility."

Gordon nodded. "You heard him, his responsibility. Go ahead."

After the machinist finished rotating the reel, we crawled out and headed to the take-up reel. There were no more wrinkles. Gordon and I checked periodically for the rest of the day. The wrinkles were gone.

That evening, after I said goodbye to Sven, I went to see Gordon. The plant engineer actually smiled at me, "I guess it was the Beloit reel. Tell you what. To save you some paper work, I'll write up the report. How's that sound?"

"Sounds good to me," I said.

* * *

Two weeks later, back in Pioneering Research, John Casey came to my office with a file and a big smile. "Remember the story you told me about what happened in Iron Mountain? Well, here's the official report from the plant engineer. You only need to read the synopsis on the first page."

I opened the folder and read.

After a careful study of what might be causing hard wrinkles, I decided it had to be the Beloit reel. This proved to be correct when, after we rotated the reel to its proper position, the wrinkles vanished.

— 5 —
The Stoic

Brad was an unhappy child: his father, incapable of showing love, would not let the mother hug Brad. "He'll turn into a pansy if you keep that up."

Brad ached for the hugs of his mother and at every opportunity latched onto her dress to get her attention. Eventually Margaret Eriksen grew tired of this constant distraction and told Brad, "Stop pestering me."

Brad stopped pestering his mother and turned to burying himself in books. What attracted him most was the certainty that he derived from books of Greek and Roman mythology. He was sure that one day an Olympian god would come and tell him that he, Brad, was destined for great deeds. This fantasy never left him even after he entered high school. Here the toughness that his stern father had inculcated in him stood him in good stead. Brad's obsession with study drew the scorn of his classmates and he had to endure numerous battles with the bullies in his school. Even so, he continued to read translations of Sophocles and Plato. By the time he finished high school, he was certain that at university he would study the classics.

Brad's father sneered at his wishes. "What are you going to do with these dead languages? You'll never amount to anything. You'll probably never even get a job and be a burden to your mother and me until we die. How can you be so stupid?"

When Brad won a scholarship to the University of Toronto to study classics, his father became even more adamant. "Why do you want to waste four years of your life studying such useless subjects? With your mind you'd make an excellent lawyer and be able to earn a decent living to boot. Get this foolish notion out of your head."

Brad Eriksen ignored his father and enrolled in the Classics Department at the U of T. His father threw him out of the house.

Brad had no choice but to sleep in the library and eat what food he could find in the dumpsters behind the numerous restaurants. Even so, driven by his love for the subject he excelled and won scholarships in each of his four years as an undergraduate. He never visited his parents again. When he graduated with top honors, several of the best universities in Canada offered him scholarships to study classics in their graduate departments. He decided to stay at the University of Toronto and in due course earned his Ph.D.

From across the country, offers for postdoctoral fellowships arrived from several prominent professors. Since he had suffered through a few uncomfortable encounters on the streets with his family during his studies at the U of T, he decided to move as far away as possible from them and chose to go to the University of Victoria on Vancouver Island.

U Vic proved to be a fortunate choice because there he met and married Charlene who was to be his spouse, lifelong friend, and support. She seemed to understand Brad's inability to experience or show love even after James, their first son arrived. Brad picked James up and even changed his diaper, but he never cuddled or kissed his son unless Charlene prompted him. Two years later their second son, Frank, arrived. Although Frank was always smiling and gurgling whenever someone approached his crib, Brad failed to show any delight in his youngest.

In the meantime, through sheer work and love of his subject, Brad had become an authority on Zeno of Citium, the founder of Stoicism. He was now a full professor at U Vic with a large research grant and received letters from prominent authorities asking him for opinions on esoteric points of Stoic philosophy. His sons were successful in their careers: James was a much sought-after construction engineer and Frank was a serious and successful artist. Life should have been all happiness in the Eriksen household, but it wasn't. In an attempt to force his sons to excel even more, Brad never complimented them on any of their achievements, but was quick to sharply criticize even the most trivial of their failings. "How could you be so stupid!" was one of his favorite exclamations. To James it seemed that he could never please his father.

When James fell in love with Frieda, a student in classics, and brought her home to his parents to show her off, his father ignored the pleasant young woman all through dinner. The young lady displayed great tact and tried to converse on various subjects of interest to the great professor including Greek and Roman philosophy. She even introduced Seneca's and Epictetus' concepts that 'virtue is sufficient for happiness'. Brad ignored her totally and stared at the food in front of him or addressed only his wife.

The atmosphere was so filled with tension that the air between Brad and Frieda seemed to crackle with electric sparks. James thought that Brad was overwhelmed by her erudition and was proud of the way she quoted from the classics. After James escorted Frieda home and returned to his parents' house to receive his accolades, his father lit into him. "You're not serious about this little whore, are you?"

James stepped back. This was not at all what he expected. "Frieda is no whore and I intend to marry her!" he shouted.

"Who ever heard of such a silly name as Frieda? I bet her family is a bunch of Krauts. You know what they did to Norway. Brad maintained a cool exterior."

"You're a hypocrite! You don't even understand your favorite philosopher in whom you have specialized. Zeno would be ashamed of you. You think that failing to show emotions is the essence of stoicism. It's not. It's making bad judgments that leads to destructive emotions. Not the lack of emotions. You're full of destructive emotions. Yes, Frieda's parents are German. So what?" James' chest heaved with excitement. Never before had he stood up to his father like this. The old tyrant needed to be told.

Brad stepped forward and before James could react, slapped him hard in the face. As James staggered back, Brad said, "What does an ignorant engineer like you know about Zeno. I am a Stoic unlike you and your artist brother. If you marry this whore, you need never set foot in this house again."

James glared at his father for more than a minute before he turned and went outside onto the porch where his brother, Frank, was waiting. "I heard what went on in there," Frank said. "Dad's wrong and you're right. Frieda is a beautiful, intelligent woman. That was obvious at the dinner table. You'd be a fool to stop seeing her because of Dad." He stepped closer to James and embraced his brother in a warm bear hug. "There, don't let that old tyrant bother you."

James' next date with Frieda was not at all like the earlier dates. Frieda seemed ill at ease and said, "Your father doesn't like me at all. He's even gone so far as to suggest to the chair of our department that I should not be allowed to vie for the Marcus Aurelius trophy."

"How do you know?" James asked.

"The chair himself told me. He also told me that he's ignoring your father's statements even though Professor Eriksen has the largest research grant in the department. I could live with your father's not liking me, but I cannot live with the idea that he would try to destroy my career. I think it best if we don't see each other again."

James was stunned. "You can't mean that. I love you and you love me. We can't let that old tyrant destroy our lives."

Frieda looked at James with tears in her eyes. "No, we can't. That is why we must not see each other again. When I marry, I want to marry into a family that wants me, not one that hates me. Good-bye." She stood up to leave.

James also stood and grabbed her. "No, Frieda. This can't be all. I want you in my life for as long as I live. I don't want to live without you."

Frieda wiped her eyes. "Don't talk silly. We're both young. You'll fall in love again. Let's not prolong this." She kissed him lightly on the lips and tore herself away. "Good-bye James."

James remained rooted staring after Frieda's departing figure until she turned a corner. He sighed deeply and turned to his car.

The next afternoon as he drove home, Brad was not at all in a Stoic mood. He cursed that little bitch, Frieda, who had deprived him of his oldest son. Oh well, I did the right thing stopping him from marrying her. What could she have brought to this marriage to further his career? He thought. In front of his garage he stopped and pressed the door opener. The door had pulled halfway open when he heard a loud bang from inside the building. "What the?" he muttered as he rushed out of his car and ducked into the garage.

There, on a chair with the back of his head blown off, sat James. A shotgun was still wedged in his moth with a cord running from the trigger to the garage door. The opening of the door had obviously caused the gun to fire.

"That bitch, "Brad muttered as he staggered into the house.

At the funeral four days later, Frank was very distraught. He seemed unable to control his tears and sought refuge in the arms of Frieda who stood behind all the mourners. She had come to say a final good-bye to her one-time fiancé. When Brad glimpsed her, he let go of Charlene and left the edge of the grave. He wandered over to Frank and Frieda and grabbing her in a rough manner asked, "Haven't you done enough damage to this family. Do you want to start on my other son now?"

Frank grabbed his father. "Leave her be you old bastard. It was you that killed him. You might as well have aimed the gun and pulled the trigger. Could James have made it any clearer than he did?"

"Shut up you idiot. How could you be so stupid?"

Frieda tore herself from Brad's grasp and walked away. Frank stared after her and then at Brad. "This is your son's funeral. A funeral you caused."

"I told you to shut up," Brad roared. Then recovering himself he said in a calm voice, 'Come stand beside your mother. She needs your support."

"Fuck off!" Frank's face darkened and he turned from his father. After more than a minute of silence, while the minister at the gravesite droned on, and the mourners pretended not to hear the argument between father and son, Frank's face brightened. He looked at Brad and smiled as if deeply satisfied. After seeing no reaction from his father, he broke into a trot in the direction that Frieda had left. Brad remained standing by himself, abandoned, apart from Charlene and the other funeral-goers.

After the ceremony at the grave, Brad returned to Charlene, took her arm and supported her to the car. He wanted to resume "normal" life. His son was dead, but that was not his fault; it was that damn bitch, Frieda.

Two days later, at his office, Brad was again working on a paper regarding the basis of Neostoicism as founded by Justus Lipsius. He was making some progress when his phone rang. "Professor Eriksen, I am Detective Elders from the homicide division. It is my sad duty to inform you that your son Frank committed suicide two days ago. Could you please come to the police station to help us clear up some details? … Professor Eriksen, are you still there?"

"Yes, I'm still on the line. When did you say he did this?"

"Two days ago."

"That was right after the funeral of my other son, James."

"I am very sorry."

— 6 —

Misfortune and Fortune

The year I finished my degree in classics with a minor in writing was filled with disaster. I looked for a job with one of the large advertising companies. Nothing. Then I looked for any kind of job at all where I'd be able to use my skills. Also nothing. I was devastated, but I still had Kerry. So, with hope and love in my heart, I approached Kerry with a small but lovely engagement ring and asked her to marry me.

She regarded me with surprise. "You didn't think our relationship was serious. It was just something to pass the time. You're fun, but not someone I'd like to spend the rest of my life with."

I could have accepted a simple, "No." But her contemptuous tone really hurt. I wandered away and the very next day left for Edmonton, Alberta. My intention was to go to Fort McMurray and work in one of the camps in the oil sands until I recovered my mental equilibrium. This would give me time in the long, lonely evenings to hone my skills as a writer. It didn't happen. My skills made me unsuitable for the available jobs and so, I took a job as dishwasher in a burger joint, in Edmonton.

After a few months the pain inflicted by Kerry grew less, and I was ready to try again, but could not find a way to approach a woman without having my mouth go dry and my knees weak. So, I stopped trying.

At work, things were also not progressing too well. When I tried to tell my boss, Mr. Marco, that he could increase business if he added some soups and salads to his menu, instead of being pleased, he told me, "Mind your own business. What the fuck does a jerk dishwasher like you know about anything at all?" He threw his ballpoint at me. It sailed past my head into the curtain covering the window in the door to his office. I turned and rushed out of the office, slamming the door behind me.

Later that day, when it was time to close, I decided that this job was not that bad. It did allow me to think while doing what I was paid to do. Rather than lose the job, I felt I should apologize to the boss. By the time I'd made up my mind to do this, everybody had already left and even the lights in the joint, except the boss's office, had been turned off.

I knocked on his office door. No response. After three taps without an answer I tried the handle. It turned; I entered, and stopped. On the floor, in front of me lay Mr. Marco in a pool of blood. I stepped forward to check on him. Nothing, no pulse, dead.

As I turned to leave, my foot knocked against a big knife. I picked it up and placed it on Marco's desk. Then, I ran.

Too upset to think, I ran for a couple of blocks until I reached the Casino. In the bright lights of this building I looked around to see if anyone was there to recognize me. To avoid attracting attention I decided to go in and have a drink. I wasn't thinking too clearly; I'd never seen a murdered person before. It occurred to me that I'd need some change for a tip, so I stuck a twenty into the machine, but it wasn't a change machine. It was a new kind of slot that took bills. I stared at the machine waiting for change, until some guy prodded me and asked, "Aren't you going to pull the lever?"

I turned to look at him, but he'd already moved on. I pulled the lever. Bells went off; lights flashed. I'd won a mini jackpot: $ 200,000.00. After cashing my winnings, I didn't even bother to have a drink, but quivering with excitement headed straight to my car to drive to my room.

The next morning I thought of staying home and calling in sick to the burger bar. In the end I decided that it would be too suspicious and went to work. Every time I glanced in the direction of Mr. Marco's office, all I could see was his wide-open lifeless eyes staring at me. At work, everything went fine. I was starting to relax. Maybe it had not happened; I had just imagined seeing Marco's corpse.

Then, John, the assistant manager, entered Mr. Marco's office and all hell broke loose. Within minutes cops arrived. They were all over the place, asking questions, taking notes, taking pictures. Then they started in on me. I was totally flustered and I guess they noticed and probed harder. Eventually they were through with me and exhausted from work and their questions I drove home.

That night the cops woke me up. They'd found the murder weapon — the knife — on Marco's desk and my fingerprints on it. Also as I dressed, one of them noted dark stains on my shoes. It turned out to be blood that matched Marco's DNA. I was in deep trouble.

At the police station they took turns questioning me until I was ready to fall asleep while standing. "Tell me again what you say happened. How did your fingerprints get on the knife? Where did you put the body? Where did you get the $200,000.00?"

I repeated my story as best I could, but they wouldn't believe me. Then they charged me with homicide. That's when I asked for a lawyer. They recommended someone, but I had money and wanted one of the best. In a few hours I was out on bail. Still, I was the prime suspect. Apparently the cops' main problem was that I stuck to my story. They asked me to take a lie detector test and I did, but they would not tell me the result. The detective in charge seemed convinced I'd done it.

For something to do I first went shopping for new clothes and then back to work as a dishwasher. Everybody there avoided me as if I had something catchy. The cops made no progress on Mr. Marco's murder. I don't think they were looking for anyone else besides me. They felt they had their killer and were waiting for me to make a mistake.

Life could have continued to go on like this — one day at a time — for quite a while until one day I'm out front sweeping the side walk when this drop-dead gorgeous blonde walks over to me and asks if I can help her with a flat tire.

She points to this shiny black Jaguar with a flat on the driver's side front wheel. I turned to her and asked her for the keys to open the trunk to get at the spare. She smiled at me in this friendly, sexy, but innocent way. I felt my mouth go dry and my knees go weak. Fortunately, she clicked her keys and the trunk popped open. I changed her tire.

After I straightened up, she walks so close to me I can smell her shampoo. "Thank you."

Despite my dry mouth I manage to mumble, "You're welcome."

She again gave me that wonderful smile and said, "I'm Nicky, actually Nicole."

"I'm Bruce, Bruce Williams." She drove off. I figured that was that.

The next day after work, as I was leaving the burger bar, when Nicky, the same gorgeous babe gets out of her Jaguar and walks up to me. "Mr. Bruce Williams? I hope you remember me. You changed my flat tire for me yesterday and I never thanked you properly. I'd like to thank you now by introducing you to some important people and help you get a better job, if that's what you want?"

Her offer sounded too good to miss. Besides, I couldn't take my eyes off her. She opened the door to the Jaguar. "Get in."

"What about my car? Where are we going?" I asked even though I didn't care as long as it was with her.

She thought a minute then said, "I'm inviting you to dinner to meet some friends. After that, I'll bring you back here to get your car."

I got into the car and we drove off to this small restaurant with sinful prices, but the most delicious food I'd ever eaten. The people Nicky introduce me to were a bit intimidating. Even though I enjoyed the food and the wine, I felt a somewhat scared. The conversation also was a little strange. They kept asking me about my ambitions and what I wanted to do with my life. They hinted at the possibility of making decent money if you got in with the right people. By the end of the evening I was ready for anything and asked them how you get to know the right people.

"You gotta get them to trust you," Nicky replied.

"How do you do that?"

She put her arm on my shoulder and said, "You gotta show them that you've got the right stuff."

Fortified by the wine, I puffed out my chest and said, "I've got the right stuff."

"I believe you," she said, "But you don't have to convince me. You've got to convince the boss."

"How do I do that?"

"You gotta show him. Anyway, that's enough for tonight. If

you're interested get in touch with me." She handed me a card with her name and telephone number. I was floating with joy.

On the drive back to my car, I asked her if I'd be able to make a lot of money."

"Sure, if you convince the boss that you're a good guy."

* * *

The next morning, I woke up with a mild headache and a strong desire to make a lot of money. I also decided that, what with the money I'd won, there was no reason for me to continue at the burger bar as a dishwasher. I didn't even bother to phone in to tell them that I quit. Instead I phoned Nicky and told her I wanted to find a way to convince the boss.

"I'll pick you up later this evening and we can have dinner together. Where do you live?" she asked.

This relationship with Nicky continued for several weeks, but I could not get her to spend a night with me. Even so, I got to trust her more as time went on. She also must have begun to trust me, because she asked me to come along on some of her "jobs". These entailed picking up packages and delivering them to somewhat shady looking characters who always paid with bundles of cash. I had no doubt that these packages contained illicit drugs.

By the fourth week I felt sufficiently comfortable to mention to Nicky that the police had arrested me for the homicide of Marco and that I remained as their prime suspect. Instead of shock, she looked at me with renewed respect and said, "Is that so?"

I said, "Yes, it is."

"Hell, if you can tell all that that to the boss, you'll get into the organization for sure."

I agreed, "When can I meet him?"

"I'll try to set it up for tomorrow. Pick you up to have dinner together?"

"Sure."

The next evening when Nicky arrived, I was ready. This was my chance to get into a large organization and make some real bucks.

Dinner was at the same high priced little restaurant that Nicky had taken me to the first time. Sitting at the same table we had sat at that time was a man in a silk suit. His bulk was most impressive. While we ate he said to me, "You wanted to tell me something?"

"Yeah, the Marco murder of six weeks ago, the cops think I did it."

He nodded. "Nicky told me."

I swallowed hard and looked him in the eyes. "I'm here to tell you that they're idiots. I found Marco dead when I walked into his office. All I did was to step in some blood and pick up the knife that killed him. Never touched the guy."

The boss looked at me. "You sure?"

"Yes, I'm sure. But I sure would like to join your organization."

The boss got up. "Nicky, you take this guy home." Then,

turning back to me he said, "Wait, I'll get in touch."

All the way back to my place, Nicky kept quiet. When I got out, she didn't even say, "Good night." She just slammed the door and drove off.

I didn't hear anything from Nicky for the next three days and tried calling her. Her number was no longer in service. I had no way of getting in touch with her.

About two months later, my lawyer contacted me. The police have dropped all charges against you. They caught the murderer. It was an internal gang hit.

That should have been it until some time after that I ran into Nicky, or someone that looked exactly like her. She was having a drink with the cop that had been the lead investigator and had charged me with Marco's murder. When I said, "Hi Nicole," and asked how she was, she looked me up and down and asked, "Do I know you?"

—7—

That's Life

Josh leaned back in his seat. The conference in San Francisco would be a success. He would present his latest results on how to start a small company and transform it into a major player. This was an opportunity to increase sales and expand from 50 to who-knows-how-many employees. Not only would he create jobs, but his employees would also have better salaries and better lives.

Later when I arrive at the hotel I'll phone Jesse. It's still hard to believe that the best looking girl in town married me, but she did.

In his luxurious suite— he still had some slight feeling of guilt about spending so much more money on a room to sleep in than his average employee earned in a day — he dialed home to talk to Jesse, just to let her know that he'd arrived safely. After six rings the answering service came on. He didn't leave a message; he really wanted to talk to his wife, not to a machine.

Oh well. She's probably just visiting Kate or one of the other neighbors.

The next day when he phoned there was again no answer after six rings. The same was true for the next two days. Josh became anxious.

I hope she's all right and nothing happened. Nothing's happened or Alfred or Veronica would have tried to reach me. Maybe not. These kids are not too reliable; parents are just another duty to them. No, I'm being unfair. They have their own lives. Alfred is busy starting a new business of his own and so is Veronica. Besides, I'll be home tomorrow.

When Josh unlocked the door to his house and after shouting, "Hello my beautiful wife," dropped his suitcase on the hall floor only silence greeted him. Jesse was not home. He searched through the house. No Jesse. When supper came, Jesse was still not home. He called the police to report a missing person.

In the morning, when he reached over to touch Jesse he encountered only empty space. Jesse was still missing. He had spent a restless nigh and was late. When he got to his office, Andrew, his accountant was already hovering outside his office. "Hi Josh, how was San Francisco?"

"Great, But what brings you to my office so early?"

Andrew's face turned to a frown. "We have a problem. Three of our bills came back unpaid. Insufficient funds. It seems the company has no money to cover its debts."

"That's impossible."

"No, it's true. I checked with the bank. Jesse withdrew all the company money on the day you left."

Josh stared at Andrew with an uncomprehending look. "That can't be. It must be a mistake. I'll check with Todd, the bank manager."

Andrew nodded. "I hope you're right. But what do we do with all our employees. How are we going to pay them?"

"Hang on until I check with the bank."

"OK."

The bank confirmed what Andrew had said. Mrs. Jessica Walton had withdrawn all the company funds as well as all the money in their joint account and closed both accounts. Todd told Josh that he had tried to dissuade her, but she insisted on taking all the money in a certified check.

"Have those checks been cashed yet?" Josh asked.

"Yes, just the day before yesterday."

"Where?"

"In Miami. I'm sorry, Josh, but there was nothing I could do to stop her. The best I could do was to prevent her from closing the accounts."

"So, how much is left?"

"A thousand bucks in each account."

"That's all? There was more than half a million in the company account and more than that in our joint account."

"I know. I'm sorry."

"How'm I going to pay my workers? Can I get a loan?"

"I'm sorry, Josh, but you have no collateral. Jesse took a business loan on your business and you already have a letter of credit, fully exercised, on your home."

"You're saying I'm bankrupt."

"That's right."

On the way home from the bank Josh realized, Jesse had made off with all his assets and left him as well as his employees with nothing. He had to find a way to keep his workers from having to suffer because he'd married and trusted the wrong woman. How was this possible? Jesse loved him. At least that's what she always told him. The idea that she'd do this to him was impossible to absorb. What was worse, all these loyal people not getting paid was more than he could face. They had to be paid. Then he realized how to do this. He would sell his car and furniture. Maybe he could even sell his house for more than the letter of credit on his house. He again went to see Todd.

"Well, I'd be happy to help you, but you can't sell without your wife's approval since you're joint owners."

"What the hell can I do? I have to pay my employees."

There's not much you can do. Jesse has you screwed. The best you can hope for is a good divorce lawyer who can get you half of everything."

"Can I sell my business?"

"Who'd buy it with all the assets stripped? She must really have hated you."

"Thanks, that makes me feel so much better."

Much as he hated to, Josh had to face his labor force. "I have some very bad news. This company is bankrupt. My wife absconded with all the assets and I have no means to pay you. You've all been loyal and good workers and I'll try to pay you as soon as I manage to sell what little I have left." It was the most difficult task he had ever had to face, and he felt like shit when a few of the senior workers said they understood and sympathized with him.

Two months later, when no payments had been made on the debt on the house, the bank took possession and Josh had to move out. By this time he had managed to sell off all the interior possessions except his prized Purdy over-under shotgun. He moved into a small apartment and tried to start life over, but he felt weak and without energy. A trip to the doctor and numerous tests later confirmed the worst: he had malignant melanoma in a very advanced state.

The expert at the university was very frank, "We can give you medication, but you cannot expect more than a few more months to live. However, if you're willing we can give you an experimental treatment, which might work. It's highly problematic with side effects. However, even if it doesn't work, the knowledge we gain may help us save future victims of this disease. Do you want to do this?"

Josh needed only a few seconds to consider. *My life has gone to shit. This way I can at least help some others and my life will have some meaning.*

"Yes, I'll go for this experimental treatment."

"That's good. You'll have to come here every Thursday for

the foreseeable future and we'll proceed with the treatment. Make sure that you get a good night's sleep the day before each treatment. That's important"

Feeling better than he had since Jesse took off because at least now his life again had a purpose, Jeff went home.

Two days later more bad news arrived in the shape of a police officer. Your son, Alfred, is in jail for drug dealing. Do you want to see him?"

Josh dragged himself to the jail where Alfred grinned at him through glass as they spoke through a telephone. "Hi Pop, sorry for the trouble, but I need help. Can you post bail for me?"

"Alfred, what kind of shit have you been doing? How'd you come to be doing drugs?'"

"Never mind that, it's a long story."

"I've got time. Tell me."

"It's that fucking biker gang, the Darling Devils. I borrowed some money from them to star my business. They were the only ones willing to lend me. When I didn't pay back on the dot they threatened to break every bone in my body unless I helped to distribute, what they called their product, to their customers. Well, I agreed and here I am. Now, can you get me the fuck out of here?"

"Sorry, but I can't help you. I'm broke. Your mother cleaned out all our accounts and left me with nothing but debts. I even lost the house."

"Fuck!"

"Stop swearing."

"You don't understand. The same guys that threatened me also threatened Veronica. If I don't pay them back they threatened to turn her into their moll."

"What?"

"A bloody biker moll."

Josh stared at his son. "I should have drowned you in your first bath. Not only did you get yourself into jail, but you also got your sister involved in your shit."

"I'm sorry, Dad. I needed the loan to get my business started."

"That's no excuse. You have to know how much you're going to earn so that you know how much you can afford to pay before you borrow."

"Stop the sermon. I've had more than enough of your shit. If you can't, or won't, get me out of here at least try to help Veronica. Where are you staying now, if not at home?"

"I have an apartment."

"Then whyn't you stay at my place. The rent is paid for the next two months."

"I'll do that."

Josh moved into Alfred's apartment and used the Internet to search for the Darling Devils to see if Veronica was on them. Sure enough, he soon found a site with Veronica featured. A man with an extraordinary big cock was fucking her. The sight sickened Josh and he turned off the computer. Those animals. That bastard son of mine. My poor girl.

The second night after Josh moved into Alfred's apartment he awoke at one in the morning to banging on his door. He dragged himself out of bed and opened the door to be faced by a tough looking unshaven man wearing a leather jacket with the logo of a grinning devil on his back and the inscription, "Darling Devil." "Where's Alfred?" the man asked.

"In jail where you assholes put him. What did you bastards do with my daughter?"

The young man's face distorted into an angry scowl. "Watch your mouth, you old fucker, before I knock your teeth out. We did what we said we'd do. Alfred owes us ten grand."

Josh stepped back and slamming the door said, "Fuck off before I kill you." He locked the door and went back to bed.

The next night — a Wednesday, the night before he again had to visit the clinic — banging on his door again awoke him. This time it was only eleven o'clock. He got out of bed and loaded his Purdy with buckshot. "Those bloody bastards are back. This time I'll get one of them." He opened the door to confront the same unshaven hooligan. He stuck the barrels of the Purdy into his gut and said, "Get the hell away from me or I'll spill your evil bowels all over the lawn. The man turned and ran. Josh rushed out onto the sidewalk. As he reached the street a cavalcade of motorcycles raced past. Josh lifted his shotgun and blasted into the night sky. The cool night air wafted over his body, and he realized that he didn't have any clothes on, Josh rushed back into the house. Several neighbors, probably awakened by the blast of the shotgun, had peered through the curtains of their houses. Josh was sure they'd seen him.

He'd just settled back into bed when he heard police sirens and shortly afterwards a loudspeaker shouting, "Josh Waring, this is the police. Come out with your hands up. We want to talk to you."

Josh picked up his loaded shotgun and placed it on the table in the room. He stumbled over to the window and peered through the crack in the curtains. The street was swarming with police in assault gear scrambling for cover behind cars. Josh did not answer the hail. Less than a minute later the phone rang. He picked it up. A very calm voice on the line said, "Hello, is this Josh Waring?"

"Yes."

"Josh, this is officer Sean Stuart. We heard that shots were fired in this area and would like to talk to you about that."

"I don't want to talk to anybody. I just want to sleep."

"We won't take up much of your time. We just want to confirm what happened."

"Yes, a shot was fired. I tripped and my gun went off. That's all. Now let me go back to bed. I have a busy day tomorrow."

"I know. You have an appointment in the oncology clinic at the university. Is that what you meant?"

"Yes, go away."

"I'm sorry, we can't. Not until we've confirmed what happened. You see we have a report that you threatened an man on a motorcycle."

He's a drug pusher."

"That doesn't matter."

"OK, now you know what happened. Go away. I've got to rest for tomorrow."

"Josh, you won't be going to the clinic tomorrow. You may have to spend a bit of time in jail."

"I see. How much time?"

"If you come out with your hands up, it'll be a very short time."

There was a long pause. The voice on the phone came on again. "You still there, Josh?"

'Yeah, just thinking. I think I'll get cleaned up — have a shower — before I come out." He hung up the phone. If I can't help the other cancer victims, my life's no use to anyone. I'm not going to spend the last few weeks of my life in jail.

Silence enveloped the house for several seconds, followed by the dull boom of a shotgun's discharge.

— 8 —
Authority

When Roger hired John to maintain the chemistry library, he was not certain that John would stay. After all, John had earned more money as a barista than the chemistry department could afford to pay him. On the other hand, the librarian job was far less onerous with more free time. All that John had to do was file the books and journals as they came in and occasionally go around to the professors' offices to remind them to renew or return the overdue books.

To Roger's delight, John settled into his job with enthusiasm. The new journals, as they arrived, were now always neatly displayed and updated. The books were properly labeled and shelved according to their call numbers. Even the electronic files were simpler to access. John had made a point of consulting Jim, the system manager to learn about computers and how to program. Altogether John's talents had been wasted as a barista and were now being fully utilized.

Roger was pleased with John's work and made sure to tell him. The other professors were also delighted with how much the library had become more accessible and how a certain (nameless) colleague no longer used his office as a storage place for books that he might want to consult at some point. John's performance was so exemplary that Roger had no trouble persuading the department to raise John's salary after only six months rather than the normal salary review after a year.

Pleased with his efforts on his protégé's behalf, Roger went to see John, who was busy in the library shelving newly arrived journals. With a big smile he told John the good news and waited for a reaction of delight. John, accepted his handshake, thanked him politely and returned to his work. Roger wondered what was wrong. John had not even smiled. The increase in John's salary was above the departmental standards and brought John's salary up to the level that he had received — tips included — as a barista. Roger followed John to the shelves where he was working, and when John turned to face him asked, "Is everything all right?"

"Everything's fine."

"Good, you've earned this. Keep up the good work." Not knowing what else to say, Roger turned and strolled back to his office. John's indifference to the salary increase bothered him; he wanted John to be happy and continue working in the department, but to do so he would need to find out what was at the root of John's problem. His first thought was that it must be trouble with John's love life. He quickly rejected that thought since only two days ago he had seen John and Elsa strolling happily arm in arm across the campus quadrangle. If not a woman, then what was the cause of John's lack of enthusiasm? Maybe he was just busy or else it was only his imagination, Roger thought. Still the thoughts would not go away.

The next time Roger had occasion to visit the library he noted that John moved with less energy than usual. His head was down and his shoulders bent forward. He shuffled like an old man. Roger did not want to ask him again what was he matter, but this image remained with him. Clearly, money was not what motivated John. So, what was it? Roger pondered this question for some time. His musings were interrupted when Ian, the foreman from the machine shop, came to see him.

"I'm sorry to bother you, but I have a problem," Ian said with his strongly accented Scottish speech.

Roger leaned back in his chair and pointing to another chair in front of his desk said, "Hi Ian, sit down."

After settling himself, Ian let forth. "I canna do me job the way I should."

"Why, what's the matter?"

"Professor Judson won't let me do me job. He keeps interfering. He gives me the blueprints for what he wants and then stays around to tell me men how they should do things. I've good men in the shop and after I discuss a job with them, we agree how it's to be done and do it. So far I've never had any complaints and nobody has ever told me to do it differently. I canna tell Professor

Judson to buzz off. That's why I came to you. You're the chair of this department." Ian paused and looked at Roger.

Roger smiled inwardly as he maintained a serious mien. He knew Judson: a micromanager if ever there was one. This would take some delicacy.

"Ian, you continue doing things the way you always have. I'll handle Professor Judson."

"Thank you, Sirr." The r in Sir rolled as if it were pebbles in a jar. Ian stood up and left.

Roger sat for a few moments before he also stood up. May as well see Judson right away before I find some good reason to procrastinate, he thought.

Judson must have been expecting him because after the usual greetings he said, "This is about Ian?"

"Yes, it is."

"So, what are you going to do about him?" Judson asked.

"Simple," Roger said. "Whenever you have a job for him, you bring it to me and I'll tell him what to do. That way you don't have to interact with him. Agreed?"

"No! How will I know if it'll be done to my satisfaction?"

If you're not satisfied with the result, come to me and I'll talk to Ian. That way you don't have to get involved in any unpleasantness with him. "

It took another fifteen minutes of persuasion, but eventually Professor Judson agreed with Roger's solution.

When Roger told Ian of his solution, the latter beamed. "So,

I be still in charge of me machine shop."

"Yes, you be," Roger said.

Later that day he considered what had transpired. Ian had felt that his authority in the machine shop had been questioned. That had been the source of Ian's distress. As Roger considered this problem a little longer he concluded that perhaps that was also the source of John's distress. The question was how to fix this. John was clearly in charge of the library, but he lacked a symbol of his authority. That was it. John needed a symbol of his authority.

The next day, Roger visited the city's largest office supply store. After much searching he found what he wanted. It was magnificent: a large stamp with adjustable printing for the date. He bought the stamp and an impressive inkpad.

Once back in the department Roger went to the library where he found John sitting in a rather forlorn posture behind his desk. He stopped in front of the desk and in a serious voice said, "John, I need to have a serious discussion with you."

John looked up. "Yes?"

"You are in charge of the library, but people do not always respect what you do. We need to change this." Roger placed the package he was carrying on the desk in front of John. "I have here a stamp that you need to use to mark the magazines as they come in. You must decide the time interval for how long they stay on the shelves before they may be borrowed. Now, no one and I do mean no one, except you, may use this stamp. This is very important. Understood?"

John nodded, "Understood."

The next day, when he saw John, Roger was pleased. John's head was high; his shoulders were back; his chest was thrust forward; and he walked about the library with an air of authority.

— 9 —

Coming to Canada

At last, the Promised Land: Canada, Halifax the city where we would land, where my parents had brought my sister and me. I expected to see Red Indians on the shore, but saw only large buildings. Still this was Canada, my home for the rest of my life. I felt excited and happy.

After being shuffled onto a train we crept for three days across this beautiful land toward the sunset. Papa had some Canadian money, but knew no English. He bought a shiny silvery bag of something we all imagined would be a magical sweet. What a disappointment: potatoes sliced thin and fried. We needed to learn to speak and read this new language, which was to become my mother tongue.

When finally dirty, and tired we arrived at our destination, the refugee camp at Ajax, it was like returning to the DP camp in Germany. Whitewashed barracks, turning grey were to be our home for the next few weeks. Bunk beds aligned against each other, so closely spaced that there was barely room to squeeze between the bunks to get to our beds. Privacy when we undressed to go to sleep was out of the question, but Papa solved that problem. It was summer and Papa used our blankets to hang them between our bunks and those of our neighbors.

There were, however, two big differences between the DP camp in Germany and this camp in Ajax: the food, although strange, was more plentiful and much better, but the mosquitoes were more numerous and much fiercer.

I remember my first breakfast in Ajax. We could help ourselves to as much as we wanted. But I did not recognize many of the things. There were huge oranges with a strange yellow skin like lemons. They were cut in half and looked and smelled delicious. I wanted to take two, but Mama told me not to be too greedy and I took only one. A good thing, it tasted terrible: bitter and sour. Later I learned that it had the strange name of grapefruit even though there was nothing resembling a grape about it. The next item I got was a bowl of yellow flakes with milk. At least I recognized the milk. It had the bluish tinge that all milk in Germany had after the cream was removed. This was called, "Corn flakes." Nowhere was there a bun to be seen, only pale white slices of what had to bread. This bread had no body to it. When you squeezed it, it stuck together like putty.

Lunch was better; Sandwiches with a fishy spread on this putty bread. However, supper was a treat: Potatoes, green beans and a whole chicken drumstick for myself. Also there was lots of butter and milk.

The mosquitoes, when we wanted to go to bed, were another story. They attacked like the German dive-bombers with a high-pitched whine that was annoying and scary to hear. They didn't drop bombs, but landed on me and bit me even through the sheet I used to cover myself. By morning the sheet was dotted with little spots of red from my blood.

Before the next night, Papa had come up with a solution. He took a towel and soaked one end; then he went for a mosquito hunt, swatting them with the wet end. I saw what he was doing and joined in the hunt with a towel of my own. After a short while both our towels were covered with the grey corpse of mosquitoes we had bagged. When we could not find any more mosquitoes, Papa covered the window near our bunk with a blanket. This kept the mosquitoes out, but also any cooling breeze that might have helped with the heat in the barrack. Before I fell asleep, my body was covered in sweat like the saunas that I'd been in back home.

During the day I roamed a small forest surrounding our barracks. I was still hoping to meet some Indians who might be willing to adopt me and teach me their ways. In this forest I could spy on all sorts of animals and even young men and women who wandered here to have some privacy for their lovemaking.

Every day Papa went to the barrack where farmers came to find workers. They often felt the muscles of the men looking for work. When one of them hired Papa, he and Mama were glad because now they could earn money and move out of the DP camp to a farm. The farmer that hired Papa was what is called a "gentleman farmer". He had been a chemical engineer for a large company and was now retired. On this farm were cows pigs and an old horse called, "Baxter" that used to be the farmer's wife's riding horse. A small stream also ran through the farm.

We were given a small house to live in. This made Mama happy because she could now cook the kind of food we were used to.

— 10 —

The Burglarproof Door

The door to the apartment was partly open. Barbara could see where the crowbar had been inserted to crush with brutal force part of the heavy wood of the door and force the deadbolt apart. The hallway was empty. It was late. She was alone. Evelyn was out of town for the weekend and all the neighbors were already asleep. Without even peeking through the gap in the door she rushed down the stairs, out of the building and across the street to the pay phone.

The police were on their way. "No more than five minutes," the sergeant had said. While waiting for the squad car, she hovered near the phone booth but also kept her eyes on the door to her building.

"Why would anyone want to break in?" she asked herself. "After all, neither she nor Evelyn had anything worth stealing. How many students did?" Oh sure, she had this old clunker of a TV and Evelyn had this stereo which she kept meticulously dusted. In fact she kept everything fanatically clean as far as Barbara was concerned. Yes, sometimes she could be a real pain about neatness and Barbara felt that she suffered quite a bit under Evelyn's nagging and constant complaining about her messiness, or her dictatorship, like making up rules for who should clean what or how the bathroom should be left and so on.

As a matter of fact, the living room had become so neat that Barbara felt uncomfortable working there. She liked to spread out and every time she tried to make herself comfortable Evelyn would "just straighten up a bit" by picking up Barbara's shoes and putting them in the closet, hanging up Barbara's jacket, rearranging the newspaper in a neat pile so that Barbara would have to search all over again for that particular ad that she wanted to tear out. When they first decided to room together they both studied in the living room, but Evelyn's neatness got to Barbara. Evelyn kept picking up Barbara's books and papers and piling them neatly on the table so that Barbara would have to start all over again and spread them out on the floor in a useful order each time she started. Evelyn won. It was too much for Barbara. She stopped using the living room for studying and used only her bedroom for that purpose.

The same thing happened with the TV. Barbara liked to sprawl out in front of the TV with popcorn and a coke. But the next thing she knew, Evelyn was all around her with the vacuum cleaner. Barbara's objections were met with, "What if someone, maybe Hank," that was Evelyn's boyfriend, "should drop in?"

"Well, what if he should? We live here, it's not a museum."

The police car squealed around the corner, lights flashing, but no siren. Barbara rushed over to the car, "My apartment door's been forced open. They might still be in there. I'm scared to go in," she blurted out.

"Alright, what number?"

"It's number ten-twenty-four, just up the stairs."

"OK, you stay here." The policeman turned to his partner and nodded, receiving a nod in return. They picked up their caps, put them on and got out of the car. As they entered the building, they pulled their pistols from their holsters.

Now more nervous than ever, Barbara waited beside the car. She didn't know what to expect: shots, screams, shouts. Slowly her fear abated and she began to feel a slight exhilaration at this adventure. After all, there wasn't much that they could have taken and here was something to talk about for days.

After what seemed to her an unbelievably long period of "ominous deathly silence" (she was already thinking of how to tell the story) she saw the elevator descend and the cop she had spoken to step out of the door and wave her over. "Come on, there's no one in your apartment. We've checked it completely, you can go up."

The living room, Evelyn's beautiful, neat living room, was a mess. Everything had been dumped on the floor: books, records, cushions from the sofa, everything. Barbara could just imagine Evelyn's reaction. The cop looked with sympathy at Barbara and said, "If you think this is a mess, you should look in there," and he pointed to her bedroom. She was almost afraid to look. She'd been working on this term paper and had all her references neatly arranged, ready to start. Now, she was afraid that she would have to do it all aver again. Anyway, she had to look, to get it over with. She opened the door and gasped. The room was as she'd left it. Everything was in its place.

Somehow, after that weekend, Barbara found Evelyn less fanatical. Maybe Evelyn finally realized that neatness was not the most important thing in life. Anyway, when Evelyn returned, from her visit home, she seemed more than satisfied with Barbara's straightening up. In fact, she commented with some surprise, "You've rearranged the living room. I like it." Also Barbara realized that since she was paying half the rent she had a right to the living room and she's been studying there since then. There didn't seem to be a problem about neatness any more. As Barbara explained, "Evelyn really has really mellowed out."

* * *

After the burglary, Evelyn's father insisted that Evelyn and Barbara get a burglarproof door. He even insisted on paying for it, which was a good thing since the girls certainly didn't have the money for the kind of door he had in mind. There was no sense trying to tell him that there was nothing to steal. He insisted, "That's not the point. A lot of these burglaries are by drug addicts looking for money to feed their habits. What if some drug-crazed junky breaks in while you're home? No, you're getting this door and I'm paying for it."

"But what about the owners of the apartment?" Barbara countered pro forma.

"I'll talk to them. Heck, it'll increase the value of the apartment."

Actually his arguments had worked so well that both girls were somewhat apprehensive about drug-crazed junkies and for the next several nights slept with one eye open, starting out of their beds at the slightest unfamiliar sound.

So they got the new door. It was a marvel of modern technology: stainless steel, two layers of stainless steel with a complicated system of tumblers, bolts, bars and other intricate devices between those two layers of steel, nine millimeters of steel covered with a beautiful enamel finish. Evelyn watched with interest every phase of the installation. First, long steel bars were set in concrete into the walls. Next came a solid steel frame. Then the plaster was repaired and painted.

"It would take at least a half an hour of hard work with a jack hammer to remove these hinges. Did you see the reinforcing steel we put over the top of them? Well, they'd have to remove that whole damn I-beam to get these hinges out. And we're putting the same sort of I-beams all around the door so that the dead bolts fit into the top, bottom, and front of the door. Yeah, I'd like to see the guy that could break into this door without breaking the whole damn wall down," the foreman gloated.

Evelyn nodded in appreciation. She could see that from now on she and Barbara would be safe and so would their meager possessions. Yes, her father was right. You never could tell what sort of crazies might try to break in, even if they didn't have anything worth stealing.

When the door was finished, it gleamed a proud brown, a strong solid brown that challenged any would-be burglar to attempt a break-in. The door was a marvel. Tenants from the neighboring apartments stopped to admire the enameled steel with the little peephole at eye level. The door was the envy of the whole building. To open the door required two keys inserted into their separate keyholes. Not only that, but "any wrong key won't turn in these special locking mechanisms," the foreman had assured Evelyn. "These are a new type of lock that can't be picked." He had proclaimed proudly and sufficiently loudly so that all the assembled neighbors could hear. "There's a spring mechanism inside that you have to push against and it won't allow a wrong key in. The key has to compress the spring at the same time as it's turned," he continued by way of explanation.

Evelyn loved the door. She loved its bold strength. She loved the solid click of the tumblers as they fell and the various bolts and bars slid into place. She loved the feeling of territorial security that possession of the keys gave her. She no longer had the fear of again having her privacy violated. That feeling which had haunted her after she realized that strangers had pawed through her personal possessions was exorcised. She felt truly safe.

Barbara was less pleased. She loathed the door and its arrogant, exaggerated locks with their unnecessarily complicated mechanisms. She hated to have to put down whatever she was carrying so that she could fumble with two keys to open those stupid locks. When no one was looking, she kicked the door, but the door remained unmarked, unperturbed, invincible.

About a week after the door was installed, Evelyn returned to the apartment with two bags of groceries and in her hurry stuck in one of the keys — in the wrong hole. She realized her mistake as soon as she turned the key and instead of the comforting click felt the key stick. It would not turn forward or backward. The spring mechanism in the lock had trapped the key. She could not believe what had happened. She stared at the key as if by sheer will power she could force it to move.

"No, it can't be," she thought. She bent down and examined the keyhole. Yes, there jammed into the hole was the wrong key. But how could that have happened? The wrong key wasn't supposed to fit. What now? In despair she sank down on the floor beside her two bags of groceries and without thinking reached inside and pulled out one of the loaves of bread, broke off a piece and started eating. By the time Barbara arrived an hour later, Evelyn had eaten both loaves of bread, a bag of carrots (unwashed) and was starting on her third stalk of celery. Barbara looked at the devastated groceries surrounding Evelyn and shook her head. "What's going on?"

"The key's stuck," Evelyn blurted out and took another big

bite of celery.

"What key?"

"The key in the door."

"Which key? What door?"

"I stuck the key in the wrong hole and it turned and got stuck. We can't get in."

"In this door?"

"Yes." Evelyn was ready to cry if Barbara uttered one word of recrimination, but Barbara herself was momentarily too devastated to accuse her roommate of stupidity. They couldn't get in. It finally sank in and Barbara wanted to rant and rave, to verbally lash out at Evelyn, but her better heart took over and she stroked Evelyn's head, "It's alright. Don't worry, we'll get in." Barbara did not really believe they would. After all, this devilish door had been designed to provide a trap just like this.

"But how?" Evelyn quailed. "We're on the tenth floor. We're not just going to get a ladder and break in. Anyway, we've got to get the door open." The tears were just below the surface.

"Look, why don't we try turning the key with a pair of pliers?" Barbara suggested.

"You can't go at this brute force. It's a sophisticated mechanism," Evelyn objected.

"Well, let's try."

It took five more minutes before Evelyn was convinced and allowed Barbara to get a set of pliers from the car. She paused with the pliers in her hand, looked at Evelyn until the latter nodded assent, and put the pliers to the key and twisted. Nothing. On her next try she felt a slight movement and applied more force. The pliers twisted and separated from the door with a stump of the key in the pliers and less than two millimeters of the broken key projecting from the hole. Evelyn had watched Barbara's attack on the door with interest, with a mixture of hope and foreboding. Now her strength dissolved and she melted into tears. "No, this can't be happening," she sobbed. "This isn't real. What are we going to do?"

"I don't know. Look, you stay here and I'll go call the company that installed the door."

Twenty minutes later Barbara was back. "I called up the company. He said they have a twenty-four hour emergency for just this sort of thing."

"You mean they're on their way?" Evelyn's face brightened.

"No." Evelyn's face clouded over again.

"Why not?"

"Well, I asked him what they do and he said they take out the whole door with a jack hammer. It takes about two hours for the job."

"Two hours?"

"That's what he said. So I asked how much."

"How much?" Evelyn echoed.

"Well, if they repair it and put the door back in, which takes about two or three days..."

"Two or three days?"

"Yes, two or three days and it's between fifteen hundred

and two-thousand bucks."

"Two thousand bucks?" The echo continued.

"Yes, that's why I told him to forget it until I talk to you."

"To me?"

"Yes, to you."

This time there was a long pause while Evelyn digested the information. "So what are we supposed to do without a door? What if some drug addict comes into the building? What are we going to do?"

"I don't know." Now Barbara could feel the tears and frustration welling up inside her. Evelyn sat very quiet, staring through Barbara while the latter waited for some reaction. When it came it caught Barbara off guard. "Damn!" Evelyn exploded, grabbed the pliers from Barbara's hand and attacked the tiny stump of key projecting from the lock. Barbara was too embarrassed by Evelyn's fury to watch the onslaught. She could not shut her ears to the brutal attack so uncharacteristic of mild Evelyn. The bit of key chattered in the door, clattered in the intricate mechanism. The whole door seemed to whisper its protest as Evelyn wiggled and twisted with all the force that the meager grip of the pliers permitted. She twisted, tortured, jammed, and wiggled with anger and fury and was rewarded with a sudden slippage. The stump of key turned and pulled out. With a look of triumphant anger she turned and presented the stump to Barbara.

Barbara burst into hysterical joyful laughter to which Evelyn added her own uncontrollable laughing and crying. They hugged each other and danced about the hallway beside the remains of the groceries. Later, inside their apartment, Barbara turned to Evelyn, "This should never have happened. The two keys should be totally different sizes so that it's impossible to stick the wrong key in the wrong hole. We've got to get one of the locks changed."

"Yes." Evelyn agreed.

On Monday they picked a tiny little locksmith store whose owner promised that he could change the lock for $65.00. Sure enough, that evening he arrived and after looking at the door asked why they wanted the lock changed. So they related their unfortunate escapade with the stuck key.

"Oh, is that all," he replied. "The next time just call me and I'll get the door open for you."

"What do you mean?" they replied in chorus.

"Oh we know these locks. We can open one of them in about five minutes."

— 11 —

The Dream Buck

Fall in all its colors was here and Hubert could hardly wait for opening day. This was the year he was going to bag his dream buck. He could visualize the magnificent spread of antlers and the neck swollen with the rut as the buck emerged from the bush. It would be a perfect shot. The mighty buck would drop without a step. Yes! This year he would get a buck like that. For many years now he had dreamed of just such a buck. Once several years ago he had glimpsed a huge seven by seven buck just before it disappeared off the cutline into the bush. He had hunted that spot for the rest of the season and even passed up shots at smaller bucks. Every Saturday he sat on that cutline from early morning until after last shot. Finally the season ended and his tag was not filled.

He prepared his gear with care. It was part of the hunt, and he enjoyed every aspect of the hunt. He made sure that his clothing was well aired. He even stuffed spruce branches in the sleeves of his jacket to minimize any possible human odors. Diane, although she did not approve, had followed his washing instructions. She had not used any softeners since they tainted the clothing with so-called fresheners.

As he cleaned the oil out of the barrel of his rifle, he shut out Diane's questions about how he could find sport in killing a beautiful animal. He had tried many times to explain to her and failed. He wasn't about to try again. She just didn't understand. There were certain things a man did. Actually, more and more women were taking up hunting. He tried to point out to her that it was no longer a strictly male activity. It was a way of getting in touch with nature. It was natural.

Finally opening day. Hubert was out in the field a good hour and a half before sunrise. He wanted to be sure that the big bucks that might hear him walking to his blind had time to settle down by the time first legal shot came, half an hour before sun rise. His blind was well placed, a couple of feet into the forest with the steep ravine behind him. It had taken him a week of scouting to select the perfect spot. Out in front was the stubble of an alfalfa field. At times he had counted as many as fifty deer in that field. This was definitely the place to be.

Hubert wiggled his toes in the felt lined boots. Yes, he had the proper gear. So what if he had to sit quietly for a couple of hours. No chance that he would get cold. The weather had warmed up in the last couple of days and he could smell the thawing earth. So far only a few leaves had come off the trees. Still there were enough leaves on the ground to make stalking impossible. Every step produced a loud crunch. To be successful you had to sit quietly in a blind. He was sure that he had chosen well. Once it got light he'd be able to admire the bright gold of the aspens highlighted by the dark green of the spruce. It was definitely great to be out here. He again sniffed the air and leaned back.

The rifle grew heavy across his knees and he placed the butt on the ground with the barrel leaning against his right leg. That was definitely more comfortable. He looked up at the starlit sky. To his right in the south were the three stars in Orion's belt. As always, they were the ones he picked out first. Almost overhead was the Big Dipper. He found the side away from the handle and followed the Pointers to the North Star. The world was beautiful. Life was beautiful. He thought back over the numerous hunts he had spent sitting in the morning or evening watching the deer. A smile creased his face as he visualized the time four fawns from two different does bounced over to greet each other. They were like children playing.

In front of him a faint rosiness on the horizon hinted at dawn. The hay bales in the field emerged as more than just black mounds. Another half hour and it would be legal to shoot. Hubert shifted his weight and relaxed. There must be deer moving out into the field by now. They usually came out from the ravine behind him. Time to relax. He leaned back comfortable in the warmth of his clothing. A pleasant lethargy spread over his body.

Something pushed against his shoulder and a voice rasped, "Don't pick up your gun." Hubert turned around to see gigantic antlers inches from his face. The buck spoke again. "Leave your gun and get up slowly. You must come with me." Although the situation was totally unreal, Hubert felt no fear. It felt strangely natural. He got up and walked ahead of the buck out of the blind. Again the buck grunted, "Now, follow me."

They headed into the bush on a game trail that lead straight down into the ravine. The trail was far easier than Hubert had imagined. On several earlier occasions he had scrambled down into that ravine and wound up exhausted and covered in sweat. This trail just wove down in a series of smooth curves. At the bottom they followed the stream to an open glade. To Hubert's surprise a number of animals were gathered in this glade.

To his immediate right were several large white tail deer. Then there were several moose. Directly in front of him was a pack of grey wolves. Next to these were two black bear. A grizzly loomed over the black bears. Almost hidden by the grizzly's bulk lay two sleek cougars. Finally on his left were four lynx and right next to him five magnificent elk.

The buck stopped and turning to Hubert stated, "You have hunted us for many years. Now we want you to understand what you are doing. You have to justify your action, not to us, but to yourself. I shall present the case against your activities. You may explain your activities. For me it is a matter of life and death. For you it is merely what? So, explain. Why do you hunt us?"

Hubert scanned the faces watching him. It was impossible to read emotion on the faces of the animals. It was like he had always noticed, the dead deer looked as calm as the live deer. What could he say? "You're game, you're meant to be hunted. All predators hunt you. I'm a predator." The big buck stared at him. "The predators in the forest hunt us to live." He pointed to the wolves with his front hoof. "They hunt us because they have no choice. They must hunt or die. You have a choice. What is your moral justification?"

Hubert considered his answer. He had never thought that it was necessary to morally justify hunting. After all, that's just something he did every fall because he enjoyed being in the woods and he enjoyed the adrenaline rush when an animal stepped out. Besides, he liked the taste of venison. Why was there a need for this moralizing? "Look, I'm a meat eater. I eat meat. I like the taste of meat. So why do I need a moral reason to hunt?"

"You can eat meat without hunting. You raise those dumb animals that do not know what freedom and life is. You can eat those. You do not need to hunt us. So, why do you do it?"

The buck was beginning to sound like Diana. There was really only one answer he could give. "Because I enjoy the hunt."

"You enjoy the hunt. Have you ever had to track a gut shot animal?"

"Yes."

"Have you any idea how painful a death that is, to feel the burning inside you and the need to keep moving in spite of the pain until you collapse and cannot move; to lie there with this burning, waiting for death to come to you?"

"No, but I always try for a clean kill."

"You try for a clean kill. Have you ever shot a doe and then seen her fawn come over to the corpse when you were gutting its mother? Did you wonder what was going to happen to that fawn during the winter?"

"Well yes, but my license required that I shoot a doe. There were too many deer. It was necessary to limit the population. That's a lot better than having you starve."

The buck shook his antlers in dismay. "There were too many of us, but there are not too many of you. How do you decide that?" The animals started to crowd in on Hubert. He was definitely beginning to feel uncomfortable. In spite of that, he pulled himself erect and stared straight at his adversary. "Look, there are more deer now than there ever were. Our farming has made it possible for more of you to survive than when there was nothing but forest. Besides, we have eliminated most of your predators." This statement elicited a low growl from the wolves, "Yes, you have almost eliminated us. Now you do all the hunting. At least we did it honestly with speed and fang. You do it from a distance sitting, hidden in a chair. You are not a hunter, you are an assassin. And you call this sport."

At this point the bears shifted uneasily and the grizzly raised his head. "You have taken away the places where we can live. If I take one of your stupid cows, your kind hunts me down." Hubert raised his hand, "Wait! That has nothing to do with my hunting deer." The grizzly growled, "Doesn't it? Why do you think we have to kill cattle? Because you kill the animals we eat." Again Hubert held up his hand. "There are more deer now than ever before."

The buck in front of Hubert spoke up. "You think that

justifies you killing us? Tell me. No sorry, tell yourself. Are you hunting us because you want or need our flesh to eat or is it because you want to display my head on a wall? Are you truly hunting for meat or is it to satisfy your ego?"

A general murmur of assent and a low growl of anger followed that statement. The animals edged closer. Hubert tried to retreat and felt something firm against his back. He tried to push back, but was restrained. His right leg was numb. He reached down to rub it and felt the barrel of his gun. Hubert opened his eyes. The sun was partway up. In front of him, broadside, less than fifty yards away with massive antlers curving forward past the tip of his nose, stood the buck of his dreams.

—12—

John's Millions

The counter and booths were empty. The waiter behind the bar looked up from his paper and pushed a saucer and cup toward me. "Coffee?"

I nodded.

"You wanna menu? You can still get breakfast, I serve it till one"

As I attacked my hash browns, bacon and eggs, a rather large man with a ruddy complexion, bushy beard and well-worn muskrat cap came in, bought a package of DuMaurier and left.

"That was John Martiniuk."

"Sorry, I don't know him."

"John, the millionaire. He runs a trap line of around three counties, about fifty miles west of here. You mean, you ain't heard of John Martiniuk?" I shook my head. "Well, lemme freshen up your coffee 'n I'll tell you. You ain't in no hurry are ya?"

"No."

"I remember it like it happen yesterday when John won the twelve million on the lottery. He come back to town 'n threw a party that nobody was sober for a week. You see he bought the ticket before he went out on his trap line an' didn't check to see if he'd won till he was ready to go out again almost a year later. You see he used to say that there was no point checking sooner cause the whole point of buying a ticket was to buy a dream and this way he could dream for a whole year for a buck. If he'd a waited another week or so it would a been too late to collect. Then after the party he stayed at the hotel here for a while before he went off to Edmonton. He never made it out to his trap line that year. I heard he made a whole bunch of new friends there, but he kept coming back here almost every couple of months for a day or two. He even bought a new pickup, a real nice four by four, but the box was on the short side. That pickup was plenty fancy with heated leather seats and all the buttons you could want. He also bought a brand new snowmobile, but somehow he kept his old truck and his old sled. I sorta thought he was just sentimental, but he told me one time that they were more comfortable, cause he didn't need to worry about hittin' nothin' and puttin' no dents in them.

"You want anythin' else? A slice o' this pie?"

By now I wanted to hear more, so I nodded. As he handed me the pie two oil field workers came in and sat down next to me. I nodded a greeting and they returned it with a nod of their own. The waiter turned to them with the coffee pot in his hand, "Hi Jim, hi

Ross. Coffee?"

A chorus of, "Sure" was followed by the cups being filled.

"So, what can I get you today?"

"A rare steak with a lot of your greasy fries and whatever vegetables you got that ain't overcooked. And put the ketchup over here."

"How's your soup today and what kind is it?"

"Hey, when's my soup been anythin' but good? Yeah, I got minestrone. You want some?"

"Sure bring me a bowl and then a couple of pork chops with American fries and some mixed vegetables. Oh yeah, fry me up a can of mushrooms too, will ya."

The waiter busied himself at the grill for a while and returned. "Yeah, like I was sayin', he kept his old truck an' sled. Then, one day he comes in here an' says he's off to see the world. He got himself this first class aroun' the world ticket an he's leavin' in a couple o' days, flyin' from Edmonton to Amsterdam. Seems they got some fancy train there called ICE, that goes at like 250 clicks or more from there to other parts o' Europe an' it's real fancy with waiters an' all an' more convenient than flyin' cause it goes from downtown to downtown.

"But first of all he's got this real good goin' away party. This lasts until the mornin' he's leaving and then he's hired this stretch limousine all the way from Edmonton and piles in there with a bunch of guys who're too drunk to stand an' off they go. So, he's gone for almost half a year. When he gets back, he picks up his old truck an' sled and heads back to his trap line. We never did fin' out what he saw on his trip, but it musta been a dandy. Now he's workin' his trap line like before, just as if'n he did'n have no millions. I guess he's seen enough o' the world."

— 13 —

The Accident

Hania shakes her head to try and clear her thoughts. The memory of the accident floods back and she sits up. Yes, there on the front seat are her aunt and uncle, slumped forward, barely breathing. She leans forward and shakes them gently. There is no response. Panic creeps into her soul and she takes two or three deep breaths the way her gymnastics teacher taught her. Her heartbeat slows and she again thinks clearly.

What should she do? This is a strange country this Canada, so different from her native Romania. The distances between towns is so great, the language so strange. Again fear rears its ugly head. She starts to shiver. It isn't only fear, she's beginning to feel cold; the car is cooling off fast.

When her uncle lost control of the car and skidded off the road, over the embankment, and into the deep snow, she had no time to be afraid before everything went gray. Now as the memory of those seconds returns with sharp clarity, the horror becomes real. She doesn't want it to be real. She wants it to be all a bad dream. She wants to wake up and find everything all right.

Her shivering increases and her teeth start to chatter. It's time to act. Her hundreds of hours of self-discipline and training as a gymnast take over. Again she draws several deep breaths and deliberately calms her heartbeat and her body. She has to keep her aunt and uncle warm. If she moves about, it will warm her up too. To begin with there's the car blanket she was sitting on. She pulls it up from under herself and drapes it over her aunt and uncle. As she moves her uncle's head a low moan escapes from him and his eyelids flutter slightly. After wrapping them both in the blanket as best she can, Hania decides it's time to get out of the car and look around.

The heavy snowflakes are drifting straight down, floating lazily and settling gently on the evenly changing landscape. There are no sharp corners anywhere; the silently falling flakes smooth and round everything. Even the scar that their careening car gashed in the side of the hill is already covered with a fluffy comforter of snow. Further along the slope of the hill, gigantic spruce stand cloaked in white.

As she trudges through the soft snow, Hania is grateful for the new boots that her aunt bought for her. She looks up at the embankment over which their car has tumbled. It seems far too steep, yet she knows that she has to get up there to get help.

She just has to get help. Her aunt and uncle need help.

Once she has started the scramble up the slope, it turns out to be easier than she expected. The snow compacts under her boots and she finds footholds where she had not expected to find any. After a long struggle she reaches the top and stands up in the middle of the highway.

Not a sign of life is visible anywhere; the only movement is the softly falling snow. There is a soft whisper as the snowflakes brush her jacket. Now that she has reached the highway, Hania is at a loss what to do next. During her struggle up the side of the embankment she warmed up but now the cold is returning. She stamps her feet on the ground and hugs herself in an effort to keep warm.

She hears it before she sees the blinking red and yellow light. A huge machine is pushing the snow ahead of it over the embankment and is heading straight down the highway towards her. Without hesitation she rushes towards the gigantic machine waving her arms frantically. The snowplow stops a few meters in front of her, the door to the cab opens and a man zipping up a parka climbs down. He's obviously asking her questions, but she cannot understand him and he cannot understand her. Finally she grabs his jacket and drags him over to edge of the embankment and points down at the car that is already beginning to vanish beneath a blanket of snow.

The man nods understanding, takes her by the hand and guides her back to his cab. She yells, "No! No! No!" at him several times and points at the car. He just nods and pulls her up into the cab. Then he picks up a telephone and shouts into it for a while.

Later in the ambulance with her aunt and uncle, she can only remember the snowflakes hitting the windshield of the snowplow, melting and fusing with other snowflakes before the blade of the windshield wiper pushes them aside. The rhythmic movement and warmth have relaxed her and put her to sleep so that she is unaware of all the activity outside until she is gently lifted. She wakes up to see a man's face topped by a fur cap. Somehow his friendly smile reassures her and she relaxes. Her aunt and uncle are already in the ambulance and smile reassuringly as she is lifted in.

It is more than two weeks later; the bruise on her shoulder has almost healed and she is cradling a hot cup of cocoa with a marshmallow slowly melting in it. Her aunt and uncle sit across from her smiling as with a deep secret. "We've got something to tell you," her uncle smiles even more broadly. "This letter just came from the government." As Hania looks questioningly at him, he continues, "You're a hero. You saved our lives and you're to be given a medal. Even better, a group of people in town have collected enough money so that your parents can come here to see you get the medal."

— 14 —
Bergisel

Bergisel is the mountain, south of Innsbruck, that boasts the ski-jump dating from the 1976 Winter Olympics. It is also the site of the Andreas Hofer Memorial, dedicated to Tyrol's great freedom fighter in Austria's war with Napoleon.

When we last visited Innsbruck our friends, Hanna and Fritz, suggested we see the Tiroler Landesmuseum on Bergisel. "Another museum," I groaned inwardly, thinking of all the magnificent hikes that I would much rather take so I could wind up at an Alm to enjoy one of the local Obstlers, (Schnapps) and a beer. I was wrong.

The museum —a museum within a museum — consists of a circular mural of more than 10,700 square feet depicting the third battle of Bergisel. To view this, it is worth sacrificing a hike and Obstler in the beautiful surroundings. The painting, created in 1881 by Michael Zeno Diemer is so replete with details that even the time of the battle (5:00 PM) is accurately portrayed. As one walks around the specially built building, the shadows depict change in accordance with the sun's position. One is put directly into the middle of the battle with the surrounding landmarks clearly visible.

The mural provides an interesting view of the city of Innsbruck as it was in August 1809.

Strewn around the foot of the painting and integrated into it are numerous utensils of the time. Here a mounted whetstone for sharpening scythes, of which one has been left lying nearby, is waiting to be set back on its legs. There the remains of a campfire and pan lie ready for use. The details arrest the eye and drag one into the action. A French officer is leading a charge against a group of determined Tyrolean farmers surrounding the Capuchin Father, Joachim Haspinger, wearing a billowing frock holding a crucifix aloft and rushing to meet the attacking French. Against a rail fence lies a wounded Tyrolean being offered a drink by a young woman.

On a little knoll beside a farmhouse stands a man sporting a bushy beard and the wide brimmed Tyrolean hat. As I admire the view, I see a man beside me point toward the knoll and say with a thick Tyrolean accent, "Des ischt der Andi" — That's the Andy. He means Andreas Hofer the leader of the Tyrolean rebels. It seems that this is the only historical inaccuracy in this panorama. Although Andreas Hofer was the leader of the rebellion, he was not present on Bergisel on that day.

The weapons of the farmers are also of various types and vintages: flint locks, pikes, spears, pitchforks and even scythes. Later, on while visiting Castle Tratzberg (another museum our friends suggested) I learned that the weapons displayed in this castle's armory are not the original ones. In their revolt against the French, the Tyrolean farmers had raided the ancient armories of the castles of their vintage weapons to arm themselves. Even so, with only their primitive outdated weapons, the farmers prevailed against the French and Bavarians.

Later, Andreas Hofer was betrayed and shot by the French at Napoleon's orders at Mantua.

After viewing all this history we took the funicular to the top of the ski hill where sits a restaurant with a fine view and refreshed ourselves with an excellent repast of strudel, whipped cream and coffee.

By the way, Castle Tratzberg turned out to also be a worthwhile visit. If one takes the train from Munich to Innsbruck via Kufstein one gets a nice view of the castle from the right side of the train.

— 15 —

Bowron Lakes, BC.

On a gravel road, parallel to the Clearwater River we arrived at the jump off point for the Bowron Lakes circuit. These narrow lakes form an almost perfect square connected by short portages, the perfect canoe tip. My wife and I had come with our Sportspal canoe and a one and a half horse motor to scout the first lake for an anticipated return trip to paddle the whole circuit.

The next morning the sun glittered off tiny ripples of the lake. As other campers crawled out of their tents to start their Coleman stoves and make breakfast we set out. The bacon and eggs filled our bellies and our spirits were equally satisfied with anticipation.

The trip starts where the lake rushes out into the Clearwater River. As the motor purred we glided across the surface, leaving an evanescing Vee in our wake. It promised to be a grand day. A large bald eagle, with a shiny trout in its talons, flew over our heads on the way to the nest we spied on the nearer shore. In spite of the cloudless sky and absence of wind, we stayed within a couple of hundred meters from shore. Just in case. A good thing too.

Two thirds along the lake the motor sputtered and stopped. I tipped the motor out of the water and we paddled to shore. There I realized that, mesmerized by the beauty of the surroundings I had not become aware of the distance we had travelled and the small gas tank of my Mighty Mite motor was empty. I refilled the tank and, after consulting with my wife, headed back. We agreed that this was a trip to be done by paddling and that we would return. The sun was past the zenith when we approached a small cove, less than two km from the campsite where we had started that morning. It was good place to stop and refill the gas tank.

As we pulled into shore I noticed several young people swimming in the lake. Four canoes loaded with gear were dragged up on shore. I understood that they were planning to start the Bowron circuit the next day and had sought the privacy of this cove instead of the campground for their first night. As I pulled our canoe onto the pebbly shore, the swimmers edged toward the shallows, but stayed with their bodies submerged. While I was busy filling the tank I heard on of the women speaking German say, "I'm freezing."

Since I spoke German fluently, I understood what she said and wandered over the beech to stand opposite them. "You don't have to freeze on our account," I said in German.

To my surprise, or should I say delight, eight perfect specimens—four young men and four young women—in nature's attire stood up and without inhibition walked out of the water toward me. The women were magnificent and I believe my wife must have found the young men equally attractive. They came over to our canoe and explained that they realized that Canada's attitudes about nudity were a lot more prurient than Germany's and that they had not wanted to come in conflict with our laws. All eight were medical students who had just finished their exams and were taking a long desired vacation in Canada's beauty.

Once out of the water in the warm sun their well-sculpted bodies must have warmed up quickly because they were in no hurry to don clothing and we continued our conversation for at least half an hour. They were indeed planning to circuit the Bowron Lakes. I warned them never to take food in their tents since this was wilderness and bears can smell food.

After filling my gas tank and wishing them a good trip, my wife and I headed back to the campground. As we cruised away we watched these eight beautiful young people waving to us. They were so natural, that I thought that they fit into the rest of the natural beauty.

— 16 —

Communists I have known

I first became aware of the word "communist" when I was about five years old. From what I could gather it was about synonymous with the words Bolshevik, Russian, and evil. At the time I also learned that Germany was fighting communists in what was that terrible country of Russia. With the certainty of a boy my age, I was sure that communists must look very different, act very different and even smell very different from the rest of us. Also, they did very bad things. My first encounter with real communists, or what I was sure were real communists, occurred about a year later, shortly before the war ended.

My mother, sister and I were staying in a small village in the eastern part of Germany. Day after day German troops marched through our village retreating with column after column of Russian prisoners. Even though my mother warned me not to go near them, I had to go see close up these evil beings that were being marched through our village. To my surprise, they looked just like our soldiers, only dirtier and smellier. Also, they looked thinner, as if they had not had enough to eat for days. They kept holding out their hands and shouting something that sounded like "Brot", the German word for bread.

When I got back home I asked my mother whether there was such a Russian word as Brot. She asked where I heard it. When I told her it was from the Russians, she again admonished me to stay away from them. Then she softened and told me that they were asking for bread. When I asked her why they would shout that, she said that they were probably hungry since our soldiers didn't have enough food for themselves, let alone their prisoners.

In spite of my mother's warnings I went down to the road to watch every morning and afternoon. Some of my friends brought a few pieces of stale bread and gave it to the Russians. In return they got little wooden toys that the Russians had carved with glass shards out of wood that they picked up along the road. In particular there were carvings of birds where the individual feathers had been carved and then stuck into the rest of the bird. I really wanted one of those. So when my mother, while boiling a big bowl of potato dumplings, went outside, I got a wooden bowl and scooped out a bunch of dumplings and hurried to the road with them. I had barely gotten within ten feet of the Russians when they were all over me. My wooden bowl was empty and I had a bunch of finished and partly finished toys. The soldiers were pushing the Russians back into columns.

A few days later the columns stopped. The village was silent. Where there had been the tramping and shuffling of tired feet all day long, now there was only silence. There were no more soldiers and no more Russian prisoners. A day or two later I heard the adults whispering in the evening around the table about Russian prisoners that had escaped and were roaming the countryside stealing and killing. Everybody seemed very scared since the only men around was the farmer who had lost one leg and two grandfathers. The next day eight Russians walked into the yard. My mother rushed out to grab my sister and me. Everybody looked scared. One of the grandfathers picked up a scythe. The Russians too looked ready to fight. Then, one of the Russians pointed at me and started talking quickly to the others. After a while one of the others walked slowly towards me, as my mother tried to hide me behind her. In a rather funny way he said, "I no hurt you. You give dumplings. You good people. We stay here. We no hurt you." So, they stayed with us in the farmhouse.

That first night they disappeared and returned in the morning with a bunch of dead chickens and some new clothes. The man with the funny language told the women to heat water "much water" and also to clean and cook the chickens. When the water was hot they all, one after the other took a bath in the big tin tub that they had carried outside and that had to be refilled each time. They were really dirty. Every time they emptied the water there was this little ball of dirt that rolled out with the last of the water. After their bath they all put on the new clothes.

They stayed with us for about ten days. Every evening they went away and in the morning they brought back food: chickens, ducks, geese and one day, even a small pig. They slept most of the morning. The man with the funny way of speaking would often tell me how wonderful his home was, how it would rain every second or third day so that the crops were the best in the world. How nowhere else was the sky so blue or the air so fresh. He made it sound wonderful and I soon found it hard to believe that these men were all bad.

One night they went away and never came back. These were the first communists I ever met. I did not meet my second bona fide communist until the last half of the 1950's when I was in high school and already a Canadian.

My high school in Toronto was Jarvis Collegiate. It stands on the corner of Jarvis and Wellesley. A few blocks west, on Church St., there used to be a bookstore: THE LABOUR BOOK SHOP — maybe it's still there. I discovered this store in my first year of high school and frequented it often because it carried many classic books at very low prices. The owner was a slim serious man who always wanted to talk politics and since I was in high school, I was very sure of myself and quite prepared to share my wisdom. After all, I had read most of Ayn Rand's writings so that I knew the merits of capitalism and was not afraid to proclaim them. Much to my surprise he did not dismiss my ideas out of hand, but listened to them carefully, even repeating some of my arguments to me in his own words to "make sure that this was what I meant." Then, slowly he proceeded to demonstrate to me the flaws in what I had stated. All his arguments sounded so much more reasonable than my own that I started to waver in my beliefs.

It was only after one of my classmates revealed to me that the owner of the store was a communist, who always ran as such in the federal elections, that it became more important to me to prove him wrong. However, I never quite managed to win a discussion. He simply had too many facts, or else was able to turn the discussion to his advantage by luring me into a different topic. Still, except for his total commitment to his ideas, he was the same as any other person. That he clearly had to be different and dangerous was brought home to me in a totally unexpected fashion.

Our high school had a World Affairs Club of which I was a member. We had a sister club in Flint Michigan and visited each other's high schools on alternate years. On one such visit, the discussion centered around Senator Joe McCarthy's revelations of the large number of communist sympathizers in the USA. I asked our visitors from Flint if any of them had ever met a communist. They all vehemently denied such a possibility. So, I invited them to come and see a real communist. They followed me the couple of blocks and stared at the sign, LABOUR BOOK STORE, peered in the window at the books like "Das Kapital" by Karl Marx, but unanimously refused to step into this store. That's when I realized that communism must be much more dangerous than I had come to suppose.

My next encounters with genuine communists occurred after I already had a Ph.D. and was Assistant Professor of Physics at the University of Alberta. The first of these was a very warm-hearted, but short-tempered professor of Geophysics, Dr. Dave Rankin. He gloried in the fact that someone, as innocuous as him, was a banned from the USA. I must confess, other than his short temper, there was nothing about Dave that made him a threat to anyone or any country. He was probably a threat only to himself since he could not resist a good argument. As a prime example of a communist he failed to meet any of the stereotypical criteria. He is one of the warmest human beings I know and, by starting a small business after retiring, even became a capitalist.

The next communist I met was far more interesting. Her name was Constantina, after Konstantinovna, the wife of Lenin, as she was proud to inform me. Her origins were Spanish and her father had fought against Franco. We met at a Physics conference in Rome where she arrived in the company of one of my former classmates from Princeton. Very slim, almost wiry, and somewhat plain in appearance she had a most vital personality that made one not notice that she was less than beautiful.

She very quickly made it clear that she was a communist and introduced me to a young man who was working for the Corriere, the communist newspaper of Rome. He was soliciting funds for his paper since they could not compete for advertising with the more affluent right wing papers. Her argument for me to support the paper was that, even if I was not a communist, this paper presented one of the few alternatives to get a true picture of what was happening. More to stop the discussion, than out of conviction, I pulled out a five thousand Lire note (about $5.00) and handed it to him. Somewhat angrily he started to tell me that this would not do. Constantina immediately stepped in and informed him that young professors did not earn very much and that he should thank me. This he did somewhat reluctantly and moved on.

Later, at lunch, the conversation drifted around to various aspects of our lives. Constantina's proved most interesting. She had spent some time in Moscow, but she had also gone to Cuba to volunteer as a worker in the sugar cane harvest. "I had to find out what these peoples' lives were like," she said. From her description the lives of these people must be very difficult. She confessed that her first day on the job she fainted from the heat and hard work. But, she lasted the whole harvest.

That evening, after dinner and wine as we walked down the streets of Rome I got carried away and started singing the International in Italian. She immediately hushed me, "Be careful! People might attack us." That's when I realized that even though the Communist Party — in fact several different ones — were legal in Italy it was nevertheless dangerous to flaunt communism.

The next morning she reappeared somewhat happy. When I asked what happened she told the following story. "Last night I did something good. As I went home I met this old factory worker. All his life he has worked in the same factory. He is quite ugly and has never found a woman willing to marry him. Here is one of the people that has worked all his life and has never even experienced the embrace of a woman other than a prostitute. So, I gave myself to him."

The most interesting communist I have ever met, also became my friend. I don't know much of his history except that he is Jewish and was born in Egypt around 1925. Later as a young man he joined the communist party and spent ten years in an Egyptian jail for his political activism. His childhood must have been quite hard, but he persevered and with the help of a kind mathematics teacher finished high school. When the state of Israel was established, his family moved there and he started university at the age of twenty-four. Eventually he got a Ph.D. in theoretical physics and came to Canada as a postdoctoral fellow. That is where I first met him.

He became persona non grata in Israel, because he took up the plight of the Palestinian people as his personal crusade. Nevertheless he remained an Israeli citizen until his death at well over eighty years of age.

These are the major communists I recall having met. None of them fit the stereotype as painted by the Nazis or extreme right wing persons like Joe McCarthy. They are ordinary people, misguided in my opinion, but definitely no more dangerous or evil than others — like religious people with unquestionable beliefs.

— 17 —

Concerts in Innsbruck

In Innsbruck, our friends, Hanna and Fritz suggested that we eat dinner in the Altstadt — old part of the city — and then go to the Innsbruck Promenadenkonzert in the inner courtyard of the imperial castle built for Maria Theresia by an expert from Vienna who combined two existing villas into one castle. When I heard that the orchestra contained no string instruments, only woodwinds, brass and percussion instruments I was not overly thrilled. I expected the typical Oom-pah-pah sounds of a Bavarian (not Austrian) beer garden. I was wrong. The transcriptions of the works of Rossini, a fanfare as tribute to King Victor Emmanuel II and recently rediscovered in the library of the British museum; Vincenzo Bellini's overture to Norma; A. Ponchielli's Adele a waltz; G. Donizetti's overture to Don Pasquale; G. Verdi's Final Judgment describing in music the path from purgatory to the final judgment; Enrico Morricone's a tribute to Morricone; Luciano Feliciani's the parade of marionettes — a modern piece composed in 2003, were all; so well done that I was unaware of the absence of strings. Under the baton of Maestro Alessandro Pacco the music in this enchanting setting kept me so enthralled that I did not notice the sky getting darker.

Although the concert did not start until 7:30 PM we sat all the time under a blue sky where the occasional sparrow accompanied the orchestra. Afterwards we went into the adjoining Hotel Sacher and enjoyed some Green Veltliner.

Altogether a delightful evening.

Three days later we repeated the experience with an Austrian orchestra under the baton of Maestro Thomas Ludescher. The music this time was totally different: Richard Strauss, Till Eulenspiegels lustige Streiche; Christobal Halffter, a modern composer who joined themes and structure of old Spanish organ music with modern elemensts; Pablo Bruna, Organ Intrada; Modest Mussorgsky, Pictures at an Exhibition. This time the orchestra contained some string instruments: two cellos, three contrabass and one harp. A particularly interesting piece was the composition that originated with an erotic song from the works of an anonymous Arabic-Spanish composer and rewritten by Pablo Bruno. This music crosses all borders between the main monotheistic religions of the region at that time.

— 18 —
Grandmother

She is much smaller now and walks with a stoop. Deep wrinkles cover the face bordered by white hair. Her hands, permanently bruised, constantly reach out to walls to steady her walk. When I talk to her, no matter what the question, she invariably answers, "Yes." It's not only her hearing, her ability to absorb information is also severely impaired. She knows this and when pressed frowns and says, "Wait, I am thinking." I resent her weakness, her old age. At one time I used to say that I would love to be in her shape at her age, but now that she is ninety-three and I am sixty-five, her every weakness is a reminder of what awaits me.

Her life has become a routine she is unwilling, or unable, to change. She must have her porridge every morning. Regardless of the weather, she must go for her walk, more of a shuffle, around several blocks in about an hour and a half. She used to vary her walk, but once got lost only three blocks from home. A friendly neighbor found her and drove her home. Of course she insisted that she knew where she was, but the neighbor said that she was confused. Now, she always walks the same route. When she is ten minutes late my wife starts to worry whether to get the car and circle through the neighborhood to find her.

Her walk is the second most important activity in her day; the most important activity is eating. Meals absorb her total attention, to the point that she is unaware that she sometimes chews with her mouth open so that I am unable to enjoy my meal with the loud noise of her smacking lips. She takes it as a matter of course that she will be served and that she gets a choice of pieces. She claims to love chicken, but does not like to eat the white meat; she must have a drumstick. Each meal has to finish with something sweet. All this is fine, but then there is the pretense that she eats so very little and would be content with "just a crust if it isn't too hard." All vegetables have to be overcooked. I hate overcooked vegetables. So now we microwave her vegetables an extra amount of time. For her, the quality of food is determined by how soft it is. Taste is secondary.

Then there is the television. We bought her a set of earphones so that she could hear, without the sound level having to reverberate the walls. They were fine for a short time. Now, "they don't work." It doesn't matter what else is on, if there is figure skating, we must all watch. The solution would be another TV. However, she insists that she won't be able to understand what is going on.

When we drive, she needs the whole back seat plus a pillow so that she can lie down; otherwise her legs swell up. She claims to love to see the mountains, but when we drive there she sleeps. It is only when someone else takes her that she tells us how wonderful the mountains were.

Actually, she tries very hard to keep out of the way. She is less of a burden than I proclaim, but I do resent the picture of my future in front of me. No, if that is what it means to get old, I don't want to live that long. I see no real joy in her life, other than the Sunday pancakes or mushy vegetables.

— 19 —

Romanian Traffic Jam

Up a steep road of hairpin after hairpin turn I kept shifting between second and third as I follow a struggling truck. Impatient drivers passed me, passed the truck at risk of life. Occasionally I glimpsed through the trees, wide valleys far below. The road entered a regrowth forest with a steep slope stretching up on my right and hurtling steeply down on my left. The truck in front braked, stopped. I halted, couldn't see past it, waited.

A flock of sheep, preceded by an ancient shepherd and followed by eleven shaggy white dogs that resembled the sheep, eased past my car. Cars followed slowly; the drivers in them smiled: a Romanian traffic jam.

From the crest of the mountain the road twisted down into the town of Jacobeni where my parents honeymooned almost a century ago. A steady drizzle dampened the romance of the lush valley with its rushing river. We drove on past Mestecanis and found a hotel in Campulung. Too much wine later we slept.

In the morning we rise to thick fog and drive on to Suceava

and finally Dorohoi, to the railroad station where in 1939 my mother fled with my sister and me under her arms. She ran from the gunfire that massacred Jews, simply because they were Jews.

Later I spent some time on the internet to find out what actually happened in Dorohoi. It was as bad as what my mother had told me, maybe even worse.

It all seemed to have started in Herta, a few kilometers from Dorohoi. There was a dispute between a Romanian officer, a Captain Boros and a Russian soldier. This was at the time that Bessarabia and the North Bucovina were traded to Stalin by Hitler for his support — the so-called Molotov-Ribbentrop Pact. When the Russian soldier drew his revolver and aimed it at Captain Boros, one of the Romanian soldiers, a certain Iancu Solomon jumped between them. The Russian fired anyway and killed both men.

"Both were given proper military funerals with honor guards. Solomon was buried in the Jewish cemetery and his honor guard consisted of Jewish soldiers commanded by Warrant Officer Emil Bercovici. A lot of Jews from Dorohoi attended. After the service a group of members of the Iron Guard arrived on the scene and murdered the Jewish honor guard as well as the mourners.

I looked into this further and learned that The Legion of the Archangel Michael that Marshall Codreanu had founded was indeed anti-Semitic, but its main thrust was against Bolshevism. The people that took it over after his murder — the Iron Guard — were nothing but a bunch of thugs. They were neither nationalists nor anti-

Bolshevists. Apparently, they were bloodthirsty opportunists who blamed the Jews for all the evil in their country. Unfortunately, Marshall Antonescu had made a pact with them and so they had a free hand to do what they wanted.

A lieutenant Gogol was in charge of a platoon in front of the railroad station in Dorohoi to maintain order. When the first shots rang out his soldiers broke and ran. Gogol drew his saber and cut the first one down. The soldiers stopped. Then he pulled his pistol and threatened to shoot all of them if they ran again. Well, his men were either shamed or scare and ready to take their fury out on whoever happened to be handy. He took his platoon and rushed toward the shooting. Without stopping to identify the actual source of the firing he picked the first building without a Christian sign — to protect themselves from the Iron Guard, Christians had marked their homes with crosses and other signs to show that they weren't Jews. That particular house belonged to a well-known Jewish family. Gogol pointed at it and shouted, "Get those lice in there! Exterminate those Christkillers!" Twenty minutes later the occupants of the building: three men, four women and five children were dead. Then he rushed back to the railroad station and continued the slaughter. Officially there were only six dead, but at the railroad station alone as I learned there were at least fifty."

The railroad station has not changed from what my mother described: a long low building backing onto five pairs of tracks. In front, an empty space fails to be a square. An ancient decaying house with a mosque-like dome on top is for sale. I feel a sense of sadness, of regret that my mother did not reveal more.

Maybe that was all she wanted to, or could, remember.

— 20 —
Sarah

Finally enough money. For four years she had denied herself all luxuries. Now, she was on her way to Athens to see the treasures of ancient Greece and enjoy the bright sun, beautiful beaches and delicate wines. Her friends were wrong; Greece had wines other than Retsina and she had read about them, especially the Boutari wines from fabled Santorini.

Although in her late fifties, Sarah still saw herself as an attractive woman. She was blissfully unaware of her vastly oversize nose and her equally oversize beam. She knew she was a sophisticated, mature woman who could handle all situations. The flight from Toronto to Frankfurt and then on to Athens was long and what with the time change she was exhausted by the time the young man met her at the airport. He was very attentive and transferred her to the hotel where an equally solicitous young man carried her luggage to her room and lingered, opening the drapes, demonstrating the various controls until she forcefully thanked him.

After a refreshing shower she visited the rooftop café on the seventeenth floor where another handsome young waiter not only showed her to a table but also held the chair "for Madame".

The view was breathtaking. Old olive trees had been planted on the roof and all around the parapet roses in full bloom perfumed the air. But, what really took Sarah's breath away was off in the distance: the Acropolis crowned by the Parthenon. This was why she had come to Greece.

As she soon discovered, the middle-aged couple sitting at the table next to her was also from Canada and Sarah struck up a conversation in which she quickly revealed her deep knowledge of Greece and Greeks. She noticed how the man kept giving knowing looks to his wife who also nodded. Clearly, they were impressed. They had been in Greece for more than three weeks and had toured the mainland to see Mycenae, Olympia, Delphi, and the monasteries perched on the steep pinnacles at Meteora. Also, they had cruised some of the principal islands. Sarah was able to tell them all about what they had seen and what she also was going to see.

During this pleasant exchange the waiter arrived and she ordered a decaf Espresso. The waiter repeated, "Espresso," and she answered, "Yes". When the coffee arrived she asked if the coffee was decaf. The waiter hovered solicitously, but seemed at a loss and finally nodded, "Yes". The husband of the couple assured her that there was no need to be concerned, that even though there was no such thing as decaf Espresso, an Espresso had less caffeine than an American coffee even though it had more flavor.

While she enjoyed her coffee Sarah noticed that one of the pigeons was puffed up and turning round and round in front of one of the other pigeons while making a loud cooing sound. "What strange behavior!" she commented. The husband smiled, "He's just trying to get her to mate. He's been trying that with every female that lands".

"Just like Greek men." Sarah had not been able to resist that barb. The husband's left eyebrow rose and dropped.

When the fatigue of her long trip finally forced Sarah to summon the waiter to pay so that she could retire, he asked, "Does Madame wish to charge this to her room or pay cash?"

"Cash."

"That is two Euros.'

"Do you accept Canadian dollars?"

"I am sorry, I can only take Euros, but you can charge it to your room."

"No, I want to pay cash."

Finally the husband offered her two Euros, which she gratefully accepted. After the waiter left, the husband asked, "Why did you not just charge it to your room and pay it with your credit card together with your room bill when you check out?"

"Oh, I didn't want the waiter to know my room number. You should have seen how he came onto me so strongly when he took me to the table."

—21—

Macho Challenge

We were hunting along the shore of Narrow Lake. The name was appropriate: the lake was nowhere much more than a mile wide, but most of the time less than that. So far we had no luck and on the way back, John spotted a muskrat swimming near some dead aspens felled in the summer by overly ambitious beavers. He unshouldered his rifle and aimed in the direction of the muskrat.

"What're you shooting at?" I asked

"That muskrat."

"Why?"

"It's a challenge, to see if I can hit it. I don't think I can, but I want to see how close I can come."

"But why? If you hit it, you can't retrieve it, and even if you could what would you do with it?"

"I don't want it I just want to see if I can hit it."

He shot and from the splash in the water, he missed by a good foot. The muskrat continued swimming unconcerned by the noise. Relieved that he had missed, I laughed. "You're right, you missed."

"Well, see if you can do better," he challenged.

I could not resist; I raised my rifle and took careful aim, allowing for the fact that the scope was two inches above the barrel. My bullet splashed just short of the muskrat, which immediately dove

"Good shot!" John shouted.

That day we did no further shooing.

A week later I was again hunting along the shore of Narrow Lake. It was gorgeous fall weather and I was stalking quietly along a game trail hoping to surprise a deer or even a moose. Birds sang in the trees. It was an idyllic experience. By and by I arrived at an intersecting cut-line that led down to the lakeshore. I decided to see if any big game had come down to drink. The shore was empty, but across the lake I could clearly see the cottage of my best friend, Alfred. He was working with Charley, his son, who was wearing scarlet coveralls. Now there was a challenge. They were across from me at the widest point of the lake. Just for the challenge, I aimed across the lake at the scarlet coveralls. In the scope I could clearly see that it was Charley. Neither Alfred nor Charley were aware of my scope on Charley. This undetected possibility was a thrill.

What if I pulled the trigger? They would never know and there was no danger of my hitting them since they were too far away. I lowered my rifle. It was a stupid idea. But what if?

Again I raise my rifle and took careful aim. What the hell am I doing? I'm aiming at my best friend's son. What if I hit him?

Yes, but the odds are way against any chance of hitting him.

I could hear John's voice, "Do it! You know you're not going to hit him. See how close you can come."

Did I really want to do this? No, even if the chance of hitting Carly was less than one in a million, I did not want to shoot at another human, let alone Alfred's son. I slung my rifle over my shoulder and started back up the hill away from the lake. Still, John's voice kept nagging at me. "Don't you want to know how close you can come?"

I stopped. That was a fatal mistake. As if something were dragging me I started back down the hill. I had to find out. Could I hit something at that distance? But why does it have to be another person? There must be something else just as far away that I can shoot at. I continued arguing with myself as I walked down to the edge of the woods. I somehow hoped that by this time Alfred and Charley had finished what they were doing and had gone inside. That way I would not have a chance to aim at Charley. They were still by the shore on the other side of the lake, working on their old tractor. I scanned the other shore for an alternate target. There was no shortage of trees to aim at. But how would I know how close I had come?

Then I saw a duck paddling in the water a little further north of Alfred's cabin. I'd be able to see the splash if I aimed at the duck. When I put my scope on the duck I saw that it was a coot. No harm if I hit that and did not retrieve it. Coots served no useful purpose that I knew. I leaned against a tree for support and took careful aim at least a foot above the coot. With the cross hairs of my scope focused in line with the bird I gently squeezed the trigger. It was almost a surprise to me when the rifle discharged. I peered through the scope looking for the bird to flutter. The bird did not flutter and I didn't see a splash. The distance was just too great to see where the bullet hit the water.

Alfred and Charley stopped momentarily what they were doing and looked across the lake toward the sound of my rifle shot. Just inside the woods, garbed in camouflage I was sure they could not see me. When they returned to what they'd been doing I was sure they hadn't seen me.

Now was the time to again sight my scope on Charley. There was no chance that I'd hit him. Shooting at the coot had shown that. Why not fire and see what happens. I aimed a foot above his head and squeezed the trigger. As I watched after the recoil, I looked for a splash in the lake, but instead I saw Charley's hand reach for his head as he crumpled. Alfred rushed over to him and cradled his head in his arms. Charley never moved. Alfred placed his head on the ground and raced into their cabin.

He's phoning for an ambulance, I thought. Then I realized what I'd done. No, It can't be true; it's got to be a nightmare. I'll wake up in a moment. But I knew it was true. I could not undo what I'd done. I'd shot Charley who had never hurt anyone or anything. Charley, who was at the threshold of his life. And what had I done to Alfred? I'd never be able to look at him again without reliving this terrible moment. I wanted to smash my rifle, but realized that this would not bring Charley back. I had to get over there to see if Charley was dead.

After racing up the hill to the game trail, I backtracked and raced along the game trail that I'd stalked before. More than two hours later I arrived at Alfred's cabin. An ambulance was in front and so was his car. I rushed in without knocking. Alfred and two paramedics were standing around the kitchen table on which Charley lay without moving. His face was ashen.

"How's Charley?" I blurted.

Alfred looked me up and down. "How'd you know he's hurt?" he asked.

"I saw."

"What did you see?"

I didn't think of what I was saying. "I saw him get hit."

"Where the hell were you?" Alfred asked.

"On the other side of the lake."

"And you could see from all the way over there?"

"Yes, through my scope."

"You scoped us?"

That's when it hit me. I'd killed a man. I'd committed murder. Well, I deserved whatever punishment the law would see fit.

"I did."

Alfred looked worried. "Don't tell anyone."

I wanted to ask why not and why he did not want me punished when I heard a moan from the direction of the kitchen table. Alfred was beside the table in three steps. "Charley how're you feeling? Just lie still and don't move or try to speak."

The younger paramedic looked at Alfred and said, "He'll be

sore, but he'll be all right. That was quite a blow he took to his chest and head. He'll be sore for a while."

Alfred let out a long sigh before he took the paramedic's hand. "Thank you," he said.

The older paramedic now spoke up. "Like Sam said, 'You're welcome.' Sam and I can do no more here. There's no reason to take Charley into town to the hospital. All he needs is rest. So, I guess we'll be on our way. If he starts to vomit after he sits up, bring him into town, but otherwise just let him rest. Good luck and take it easy."

The two paramedics picked up their gear and left the cabin. Alfred now turned to me again. "You mean to say you saw from all the way across the lake how that goddam tractor's roll bar hit Charley in the head?"

"No, I didn't see that."

"Then, what exactly is that you saw?"

"I saw Charley reach for his head and crumple."

"That's it?" Alfred sounded both incredulous and relieved at the same time.

"Yeah, that's all."

Two weeks later, Charley was all recovered. He had not suffered any lasting effects as tests confirmed. I, on the other hand, could not recover from my close encounter with disaster. I sold my rifle and shotgun and have never again fired a shot from that day.

— 22 —

Meanook Centennial

It was an old wooden shed with the roof falling in. Long abandoned and fallen into disuse, whatever its use had once been, along the highway to our cottage north of the town of Athabasca, I found this picturesque ruin and took several pictures of it. At the time I was simply fascinated by this structure and had no idea that it would lead me to meet some very interesting people. Eventually I used this photograph as the cover to my book of short stories.

After **The Jacket and Other Stories** was published, my wife urged me to find out who owned this interesting building and give them a copy of my book. After searching through the county map I learned that the owners were Tom Krawiec and Jan Baker. Although we stopped several times at their house on the way to our cottage to deliver a copy of my book, we never found anyone home except for a very pregnant cat, a friendly Doberman and another large friendly dog of nondescript breed. Then one day as we were about to again leave in disappointment, a rather attractive woman hailed us. It was

Jan. After introducing my wife and me, I explained our presence and handed her a book. She seemed delighted and we chatted for some time. According to Jan, Mrs. Smith, a lady in her eighties is a virtual encyclopedia of the history of this area. Jan even offered to introduce us to her, but then she had another idea. On the long weekend in August, Meanook would be celebrating its 100th Anniversary. This would be an ideal time to meet some of the oldest living residents of this area and hear their stories. She also mentioned that the original owner of the land, on which the ruin was located, was a Mr. Plante and his grandson, George Plante lives in Athabasca. She even gave us a copy of the June 3 edition of the local paper, the **Town&Country,** in which the centennial celebration was featured.

Once home, we carefully noted the date, August 2 to 4, in our calendar and planned to attend. As it turned out, our granddaughter with her two children came to visit her mother, our daughter, in Evansburg on that weekend. We had to change our plans. On Saturday we went to Evansburg to visit with our granddaughter and our great grand children.

On Sunday I drove to Meanook. I had missed the banquet, but arrived at the end of the pancake breakfast where I had the good fortune to meet the daughter of Ed, the oldest resident of Meanook. He is a magnificent figure of a man: erect, clear eyes, firm voice, powerful hands. Ed invited me to join him and his two friends, Mike and Allan at their table for coffee. Allan is a short, wiry man — all sinews and muscle. The first thing I noticed about him was his infectious smile. The fact that he had no teeth did not in any way diminish his smile. His eyes sparkled with energy. In spite of his age, he seemed unable to sit still and vibrated with energy. He said he didn't have much to tell, but he did and he told it with zest. Mike is a taciturn man with a big frame and a large chest. He exudes friendliness and self-confidence.

These are their stories.

Ed's Story

At first Ed reminisced with obvious nostalgia about how wonderful life was in the early days when he was a young man. He leaned forward and started his story in a soft voice.

When I was a boy, my dad got three milk cows and every day we separated the cream. I loved the sound of that separator when I cranked the handle. Every morning at five I rode a horse to the rail line with a big milk can full of cream balanced on the saddle horn. Later in the day when I got home from school, I'd pick up my 22 and head into the bush. I usually came home with something for the table. We ate real good. All of it was grown or raised on the farm. None of this crap you get fed now.

Talking of good eating, the best was harvest time. Threshing was a time of hard work, forking the stooks, but it was also a great time. Neighbors came together. We had six meals a day. At ten the women brought us lunch. Then they brought us coffee. At twelve they brought supper. Later we had two more meals. At that time I was as strong as a bull. I could lift a full barrel of gasoline. Not now.

Those women sure knew how to cook.

In the summers I worked on the farm and in the winters I went into the bush to work in a lumber camp. Yeah, those were good times, but most of he people I knew are dead now. But it wasn't all good times.

I remember coming home one evening and I'd just taken off one boot when I heard this woman screaming in front of our door. I rushed out with only one boot on and there in front of their dusty Pontiac stood Mrs. Brown, our neighbor's wife, screaming her head off. In the car all burned, with his nylon shirt melted into his skin was her husband. One glance and I knew he was in a bad way. I yelled to my wife to call the hospital to make sure a doctor and ambulance were there. Then, I jumped into the Pontiac and hit the gas pedal to the floor. As I raced away I could see the smoke from their house. It was going up in flames. I didn't care; I had to get him to the hospital

On the main road to Athabasca a RCMP spotted me and, with his lights flashing and his siren howling, followed. I just kept the gas pedal to he floor. After I turned into the hospital emergency lot he turned his lights and siren off. When he got near the car he said, "Eddy that was quite some driving, I could barely keep up with you."

"Take a look in the back seat and you'll see why I drove like I did," I told him.

By now two nurses had come out. They wanted to pick Brown up to lift him onto a trolley. I yelled at them to stop and get a doctor and the ambulance people. Didn' they see that his burned skin would come off in their hands? They got the ambulance guys who knew what to do. They got a blanket under him and lifted him into the ambulance on that blanket. If those nurses had touched his body, I don't know if he would have survived. I'm sure his skin would have come off in their hands. Then the ambulance took off and drove him over the gravel highway 140 km to the hospital in Edmonton. Can you imagine two and a half hours of bouncing on a gravel highway with your body all burned? Later when I visited him in the hospital, he told me, "Eddy you did a real good thing for me when you didn't let those nurses pick me up."

He was in the burn unit for almost a year. At first they thought he wouldn't live; his burns covered most of his body. But he was a tough bird; he even outlived his wife. He's dead now. He told me how the fire got started.

"We'd bought a new dryer and I hooked it up to the propane line, but I must not have gotten the connection tight enough, cause it leaked and blew up, blowing me right out of the house. Otherwise I'd have burned to death together with the house."

We don't fit into this world no more. Ed stopped speaking and looked at his companions who, like me, had listened attentively while he spoke. Now they nodded.

Allan's Story

There was the time we was having a big get together. Jimmy said he'd make a rabbit soup for us if we got some rabbits. Well there was a lot of rabbits in the area and I set out some snares. The next morning I had six. He used them all and made a big stockpot of soup. Everybody thought it was too much, but when we were done eating, the whole pot was empty.

I remember when my sister got married. I didn't know the family she was marrying into at all. I had to find out what kind they were. Her future brother-in-law was standing outside the church, waiting to greet everybody. I walked up to him and asked, "Have you ever eaten rabbit?"

He looked at me with a shocked expression and said, "Eaten rabbit? Hell, we ate so much rabbit that every time our dog barked, we hid under the porch."

I stuck out my hand. "Welcome to the family."

Nowadays people don't know what it means to be poor. Also, nowadays it's easy to travel, even to get around in the bush. I've now got skidoos in the winter and an Argo in the summer. It's mostly muskeg up north where my trap lines are. That's why I use an Argo, not a quad. When I was younger, we didn't have these machines. In the winter I used to get around in the bush on skis. At first I took snowshoes, but they got caught in the willows and it was a bitch to get them untangled. With skis I never got tangled; they went over the top of the willows as well as the logs. Yeah, they were about seven feet long and that kept me from sinking in.

These days the price of furs isn't as good as it was a few years ago. This business of cutting trade with the Russians over this trouble in Ukraine has really hurt the fur market. The Russians used to be our best customers. Now we can't trade with them any more. The only fur that's still got a reasonable price that makes it worthwhile to trap is coyotes, I don't know why, but they even bring a better price than lynx.

In the bush I eat moose. I've tried different animals I trap. Muskrat's pretty good. I just eat the hindquarters — they're like chicken. I don't like squirrel; they're too gamey for my taste. The Indians tried to get me to eat beaver, but I never developed a taste for them. The best eating is ruffed grouse. Then there's ptarmigan; they're a lot like spruce grouse. Not bad. Ruffed grouse are best in the fall when they've been eating rose hips and high bush cranberries. That's real good eating.

Yeah, I done real good trapping. I also worked in the oil patch for a while until one day, at the rig I was working on, the monkey pad broke. That's the pad high up on the rig where the guy stands and tilts one of the vertical pipes so the crane operator can get it in line to screw on to the next section. It shouldn't have happened, but in those days there weren't many safety rules. The whole rig was on a tilt that day cause heavy rain had washed part of the base away. After some discussion the guys in charge decided to go ahead anyway; it was the least expensive thing to do. Then, because of the tilt, the monkey pad broke and all these vertical pipes came crashing down around me. They broke my ribs, my legs and my neck. I was laid up in a hospital for more than six months. I'd had enough of the oil patch and went back to trapping. Now I'm retired, I'm 78.

At this point Mike broke in. "Retired, my foot. He's still trapping."

This speech seemed to break Mike's silence and he opened up. Until this time, he'd sat without speaking. When I mentioned to him that he hadn't said much and that he also must have some story to tell, he said, "I don't remember any." However, remember he did and this is his story.

Mike's Story

For a while I worked for El Dorado mines on the shore of Great Bear Lake hauling timber for shoring up the mine. I did this for six winters with a Linn tractor, pulling up to a dozen sleighs loaded with timber. The Linn's a tracked vehicle with tracks in the rear and wheels in the front. It's great for going in a straight line, but not much good if you need to make a sharp turn. These logs we hauled were 16 foot long timbers: from 4 to 6 inches they were called lags, from 6 to 9 inches they were stalls, and from 9 inches up they were logs that were used for lumber. We had to load these by hand. These sleighs were loaded pretty high, not an easy job. You had to be strong to lift these logs that high.

I was pretty good friends with the Indians. One time I needed to get somewhere I'd never been. There was an older Indian and his son who wanted to go near there. I said I'd take them, but they'd have to ride in the caboose. "When I slow down," I said, "You have to tell me which way to go." They agreed. Every time I slowed down, the young Indian stuck his head out the window of the caboose and pointed, "That way, that way." I got to where I needed to go and so did the Indians. I remained good friends with the Indians and that saved my life.

He stopped and looked at me and asked, I suppose you know what a pressure ridge is? Well, these gaps in the ice open up in winter when it's real cold and then later the wind blows them together again to make ridges in the spring. This one time we were starting to head across Great Bear Lake to El Dorado with a dozen sleds behind my Linn when we come across an open pressure ridge. I drove along the ridge to one side hoping it would get narrower, but it got wider. I then swung around in a big circle and headed back. "Well boys," I said, "We're gonna spend the night here." It dropped to around minus forty during the night.

The next morning I said, "We got to get to El Dorado to get bigger logs to cross that ridge." El Dorado was forty miles away across the ice. Since I was in charge I couldn't ask one of them to go. The open ridge had frozen during the night, but I couldn't risk the Linn. We had six cans of beans between us. I took four of the cans and headed out across the ice. It was nine o'clock.

I just kept walking, even when my legs hurt. A couple of times I lay down on the ice, but soon got up again and kept walking. I made it to El Dorado by seven the next morning. After they loaded a sleigh with logs and put a cat on a second sleigh we headed back. I slept all the way. At the ridge we slid the logs across the frozen ridge and pulled the Linn and other sleighs across. The ice over the gap by then had frozen to a depth of eight inches, but we couldn't risk losing the Linn. It all ended well. Not so well another time.

I again was pulling a load of twelve sleighs loaded with timber across the ice. We were almost to the other side — no more than five or six miles from El Dorado when we hit a small open ridge that had froze back over so we couldn't see it. The wheels and tracks on one side of the Linn hit the new ice and broke through, tossing Jim and me as well as one of the sleighs into the open water. Down I went into thirty feet of water. The shock was something else, but I told myself, "You've got to get up." I swam up. When my head popped above the surface the cold water started rushing in past the collar of my parka. That's when I told myself, "I'm up and I'm staying up." I yelled for Jim. He said, "I'm up, but I can't help you, I'm caught between some logs." I made my way round to the other side of the logs and pulled myself up. You won't believe how strong you can be in a situation like that. I reached out and with one arm yanked Jim right out of the water and tossed him on top of the logs.

That's when I remembered what the Indians had told me. "If you ever fall though the ice, roll in the snow. It'll stick to your wet clothes and soak up all the water and help keep you warm." I yelled at Jim. "Roll in the snow."

After that I said, "Let's get to El Dorado." I started running, with Jim following. He was a heavy smoker and couldn't keep up with me. I just kept running until I got to the camp.

I remember that when I got into camp the first thing I saw was an Indian with a Swede saw cutting firewood. He knew right away what had happened, cause he flung that saw away and came to help me. I yelled, "Get Jim. He's behind me." Then I stumbled into the cook shack and collapsed.

Sometime later they brought in Jim. He was all right. I guess the Indians telling me to roll in the snow saved our lives.

When Mike finished his story, Allan asked one of the passing women when the concert inside the hall would start. She told him that it had started a half hour ago. He rose to go inside the Meanook Community Hall, built in 1928. Allan said he was going in to listen. I said I'd follow. Ed and Mike said they were leaving. Allan promised me that he would get his daughter-in-law to send me the recipe for rabbit soup. We shook hands and parted.

— 23 —

Meeting by Chance

Last month I bumped into myself. It was hot and the street was crowded and I was trying to get to the ice cream vendor. Then I bumped into myself. I mean, there I was staring at myself, staring at myself, face to face with myself. We, I, had been trying to get to the ice cream counter, both of me. I was — we were — trying to be with both my, our, bodies in the same place at the same time. I could not tell which me was me. The moment lasted only seconds, definitely not minutes. I either merged into one or somehow separated into two entirely separate beings. One moment I was two; then Joan called my name and I answered as one.

I thought for a while — only a little while — that my mind had played tricks on me. It could have been just the surroundings, the Eaton's Centre with all those mirrors and things. That's why I didn't say anything. I sometimes feel almost disoriented there. But then strange things began to happen. Strangers started talking to me as if I was supposed to know them and people I knew acted like strangers. I knew their names, addresses, names of their spouses, little details of their lives all of which I told to them when they claimed not to know me. They only looked at me as if I was nuts. That's why I flew out here to visit you. I know we haven't seen each other for years and you can't imagine how glad I am that you haven't changed.

I mean, take Joan, the same one that was with me when this first happened. I've known her for years. We met purely by chance at a party; it was one of those spur-of-the-moment decisions to go to the party and there she was. We dated on and off since then. It never amounted to much, but we became pretty good friends. Yet, when I met her again the other day, it was almost painful.

"Hey Joan, how are you?"

Instead of answering she just walked away from me. I ran after her and grabbed her arm, "Hey Joan, Joan. Didn't you hear me?"

"I'm sorry, I don't know you." She actually looked annoyed and kept staring at my hand on her arm. So I let go and she rushed away. Again I ran after her, "Come on Joan. What's going on? Don't pretend you don't know me. We've been friends too long for that."

"Look Mister, if you don't stop bothering me I'll scream." She really looked scared and ready to scream. I didn't know what to do. I tried again, "Come on Joan, what's going on? You know I know you. You live at 317 Birchcliffe, you have a room mate named Agnes and you work at Eaton's in the accounting department as a computer analyst." Now she looked really scared.

"Look, I don't know how you know all this about me, but you'd better leave me alone." With these words she turned and actually ran. Yes, ran. What could I do? I just watched her disappear into the crowd.

These sorts of things have happened more than once so I started to look into all sorts of strange things. Somebody suggested it might be that I had a Doppelgänger. Hell, I didn't even know what that was. It turns out that this is supposed to be somebody that is you and takes over part of your life. But if that was so then I would have had to be the Doppelgänger otherwise none of it made sense. I spent days over at the University library reading up on this stuff. Well, it turned out to be just a lot of crap. There isn't any real evidence for any of it. Sure, there are people who look like you. But people who are you? No chance.

It was at the University library that I ran into this nut. He saw what I was reading and asked me about it. At first I pretended I was just reading for curiosity, but after a while I began to realize that he knew a lot about this stuff so I started to confide in him. He explained a lot of the more difficult things to me and showed me why it was just a bunch of hooey. Then he suggested something even crazier. I mean really crazy. It turned out that he was a theoretical physics prof and had this weird notion of reality. He suggested it might have something to do with some guy Everett's interpretation of Quantum Mechanics. He started to explain it to me and then he sort of lit up and told me that he was going to give a talk on it. I think he just wanted one more body in the audience. Anyway, that's how I happened to listen to him expounding on Everett's **Many**

World Interpretation of Quantum Mechanics.

Most of it was just plain gibberish. He drew a lot of little diagrams and talked about, "Double Slit Experiments," which I never found out whether they were real or just made up because he kept also talking about, "Gedanken Experiments," which were definitely not real. He was trying to explain this theory of Everett's and kept referring to the fact that, "The wave function describes the probability of a measurement being observed, but that of course in any given observation, that particular observation is realized with 100% probability after the event. What the wavefunction determines is the probability of finding oneself in the universe where this observation is realized." I mean, here this guy was saying that every time an atom did something, which could go more than one way, the universe split and in one version the atom did one thing and in the other it did its other thing. So according to Everett there are zillions and zillions of copies of the universe in each of which, one of every possible thing has happened. Can you imagine, in one of these universes there's a copy of me that has won the Lotto 6/49. What bull! What a hell of an idea!

Anyway, so it went until the day before yesterday when I went back to the Eaton's Centre, where Joan and I usually went every Saturday just to walk around, where the whole damn thing started in the first place. You won't believe it, but suddenly there I was staring at myself staring at myself again. Then something happened and when I looked again my other self, who had been beside me a moment ago, was gone.

On the way out I met Joan. She smiled at me and started to walk over to me. But I didn't smile back. I sort of recalled my incident with her and I remember thinking that I knew all those things about her, but now I was pretty sure that I didn't really. Anyway, I just turned and walked away as if I hadn't seen her. I told myself I didn't want her to start screaming or something. But the truth is I was scared. Then she called after me, "Hey Frank, remember me? What's the hurry? Where are you off to this time?"

This was really disturbing. I mean, a couple of weeks ago she'd acted as if I were a total stranger and now she knew me. I turned back and asked her why she'd acted like that. She smiled the way I remembered when she found something really funny. "Come on Frank, what kind of stunt are you pulling this time. It's you that's acted funny the last couple of times we've met. You're the one that acted as if you didn't know me." Then she proceeded to tell me about our last two meetings where I was supposed to have pretended not to remember her name or anything else. It didn't do any good denying that it hadn't been me. She thought I was playing some sort of game.

I've thought and thought about all this and maybe this guy was right about Everett's many worlds. Maybe there are many copies of this world and for a short time the two copies of me somehow switched places because in both of these worlds things became identical where we were. I don't know; it all seems so far-fetched. But y I know it happened and there's nothing wrong with me.

— 24 —

Liesl

I must have been about fifteen years old, back in 1951, the first time I saw Liesl. Frank had brought her over to Toronto from a small town in Austria to be his bride. She was a petite woman with a lively expression and blond hair that descended to her shoulders in long curls. Her shiny red mouth was always smiling and I immediately longed to kiss those lips. I thought she was gorgeous and much too pretty and far too young for Frank, who was at least thirty-five years old.

Whenever I was close to her so that I could smell the faint perfume of her, I had to hold my breath until I almost ran out of air, to avoid getting an erection. But I did get to kiss those lips — even more than once.

For three weeks, while waiting for the wedding to happen, Liesl stayed in my parents' home. Two blocks away, a huge white lilac stretched over a fence into the back lane. With the romantic notions of a young teen-ager I dreamed of wooing Liesl and cut a bouquet of lilacs from the branches hanging into the back lane. My dreams were fulfilled. When I presented the lilacs to Liesl, she kissed me.

Overwhelmed I rushed back down the lane and gathered another bouquet. Again she kissed me. This time as she embraced me I even felt her breasts pushed against my chest. It was ecstasy and I didn't even care that I became erect. Her lips and breath were everything I had expected. Over the next three days I returned time and again to the lilac bush and continued to be rewarded with Liesl's smiles and kisses. To my delighted surprise, her lips lingered ever longer on mine.

I was sure she loved me. Then she married Frank.

A few months after the wedding, my sister, Liesl and I took the ferry to Center Island and walked to the beach on the side away from the city. Without hesitation, Liesl stripped away her dress to reveal the skimpiest bikini I had ever seen. I could not tear my eyes from this display of so much feminine charm. I was not the only one. In minutes, a man approached and began a conversation with Liesl who seemed delighted. I was more than a little upset. It was bad enough that she'd married Frank, but now she was also flirting with this strange man.

I saw that my sister was also displeased. She kept trying to draw Liesl into a conversation and tried to push me between Liesl and the stranger, but Liesl was having none of that, edging past me to stand so close to the stranger that I could not insert myself between them. Eventually my sister managed to drag Liesl away by saying, "We have to go; your husband will expect us." Liesl shot her an unpleasant look and the stranger left.

We stayed on the beach, but my day was spoiled, especially

after Liesl asked my sister, "Why did you chase that man away? He was quite good looking."

"We're married women," my sister answered.

"Yes, but that doesn't mean we can't have some fun," Liesl said.

I couldn't believe my ears. This beautiful woman of my dreams didn't care that she was married. She was not the pure maiden I imagined.

My next memorable encounter with Liesl was two years later. By now I was seventeen with raging hormones and all my thoughts dwelling on my desire to lose my virginity. I no longer dreamed of pure maidens; I dreamed of a willing maiden, one that would turn my wet dreams into reality. My parents and I, together with Frank and Liesl had been invited to my sister and her husband, Patrick's, home. After and during the barbecue, the adults had been tossing back one cocktail after another. The party grew livelier.

In a lull, while my mother had gone inside, Patrick turned to me and asked, "So, John, when are you going to finally lose your virginity?"

I spluttered, "I'm not a virgin." At the same time I could feel my face redden.

They all laughed and I wanted to hide. That's when Liesl turned to me and said, "That's nothing to be ashamed of. Why, most women would be willing to help you."

"Would you?" Patrick asked.

"Yes, would you?" Frank echoed.

"But I'm married. . . . Would you care?" Liesl asked Frank.

Frank got up and walked away. Patrick pulled twenty dollars from his wallet and reached across to me. "Here's enough money for two people to stay at a good hotel. Here's your chance." Then turning to Liesl he continued, "Well, Liesl, are you still willing to help John lose his virginity?"

My sister looked shocked.

I could not believe that this was happening. My dreams were again turning to reality. I could see myself with Liesl in a large bed. It would be marvelous. But, before Liesl could answer, my father spoke up. "This has gone far enough. Patrick put that money away and then apologize to Liesl and Frank." Turning to me he continued, "John go find your mother. It's time to go home."

So, I did not lose my virginity that night, even though I came close. Frank and Liesl's marriage broke up after less than a year.

The next time my sister was over at my parents I heard her explain to my father that Patrick had done what he did that evening because he knew that Liesl was unfaithful and he wanted Frank to know.

As for me, I did eventually lose my virginity, but that's a different and private story.

— 25 —

My First Real Drink

My first trip to a bar occurred when I was about fifteen or sixteen. It was on a Saturday. At four o'clock I'd finished work at Eaton's, and was walking up Yonge Street toward Dundas when I met Alexandru. I knew him from the Romanian Club to which my parents often dragged me. Alexandru was in his mid twenties, a slim, handsome man with brown eyes and shiny, pitch-black hair. He was in the company of George, another man, about the same age as Alexandru.

After introductions, they invited me to join them for a drink. I'd had wine at home, but never a cocktail. I mentioned my age to these men, but Alexandru assured me that with my size — I was already tall — it would be no problem. We continued walking up Yonge until we reached BASIL'S TAVERN, where we entered. Alexandru and George ordered Scotch for themselves and a Tom Collins for me. The taste of the drink was delicious: something like lemonade. When we left the tavern I felt happy and wonderful.

George suggested we go to his house, he needed to be home since John, his four-year old son, was due to wake up, and we could continue drinking there. On the way they stopped at an LCBO store and bought liquor. George's apartment was modest, but neat. I learned that his wife was at work and George was looking after John. The men poured generous portions of alcohol into glasses and I drank bravely to keep up with them.

After we'd had several drinks, I heard timid footsteps padding down the hall. George rose. "John's awake," he said and staggered to the hall. I heard two loud slaps — a loud 'Ow', but no crying — and George saying, " No crying or Ill give you a reason. Now, get your potty and sit on it. Don't move till I come back to get you."

George returned and picked up his drink. "Sorry," he said.

The drinking continued. Time passed and even though it was summer, I could see it getting darker outside when George turned on the lights. I felt uneasy. I could not imagine having to sit on a potty like the little boy, John, was doing without reprieve. It had to be uncomfortable and painful. I did not know how to help the little boy and wanted to get away.

"I have to get home before my parents worry too much about what happened to me," I said.

"In that case, you'd better go," Alexandru said.

George nodded. "Yes, go. Besides, Margaret should soon be coming home."

I thanked both of them and left. I felt sorry for John , even though I'd never met him. How could a father be so cruel to his son. I wondered if the alcohol affected his feelings. I'd felt good with that first drink. Now I just felt woozy and sorry.

— 26 —

Opening Day in Italy

Every fall millions of birds cross from southern France over the Ligurian Sea to the coast of Italy somewhere in the vicinity of Piombino south of Leghorn. It is a time greatly anticipated by thousands of Italian hunters. The flocks include a variety of ducks as well as large numbers of songbirds, all of which are a delicacy greatly prized by the mighty Italian hunters.

On opening day, when these multitudes of birds, exhausted by their long flight, are due to arrive on the Italian shores of the Tyrrhenian Sea, a great host of hunters assembles on these shores. They are there to repel this invasion of hungry birds and to prove to their spouses that they have what it takes to feed a family.

For weeks now these hunters have cleaned their shotguns, made sure that they have an adequate supply of lead cartridges, clean hunting uniforms, and an adequate supply of well-aged grappa.

The great day arrives. The hunters in their excitement have been unable to sleep the night before, in fear that they might miss the early rising to get to the shore before the other hunters. Finally the alarm rings and, over their wives grumbling complaints, they get out of bed, wash dress, and turn on the Espresso machine. After an espresso, corrected with grappa, and a sweet roll they are ready to head out.

Those living close to shore have an advantage. Those coming from further inland have to cope with roads congested by idiots dressed in hunting gear, heading seaward at this early hour before there is even daylight. Parking is another problem that only cause a few dented fenders and incensed tempers.

Finally the armed host is assembled, in an array three deep on the shore, ready to face the invading squadrons. There is the soft murmur of the voices of men waiting in anticipation. Slowly, ever so slowly, daylight creeps over the dark sea. No birds. When the sun peeps above the horizon behind the hunters, the sea sparkles in all its purple glory, the color of a warm Barolo. It reminds the hunters that they have to fortify themselves for the impending challenge.

More than two hours later, far out over the Tyrrhenian Sea a dark cloud begins to approach. The hunters double check to make sure that their shotguns are really loaded and that their thumbs are poised over the safeties. They hold their weapons loosely cradled in their arms waiting for the cloud to approach so that individual birds may be distinguished. Soon after that the birds will be in range. To no avail.

Someone in the first row cannot wait. He raises his musket and fires when the birds are still far out of range. This is a signal. All the hunters raise and discharge their weapons. The shot drops harmlessly into the sea. The birds, shocked by this unexpected thousand-gun-salute, gain altitude. The cloud continues coming and passes over the hunters, well out of range of their weapons.

After the flocks have passed, the hunters dispirited by their lack of an ample supply of grappa and success, head back to their cars and homes. But, the Italian hunting spirit is not that easily extinguished. On the way to the cars, anything that pops up, be it a butterfly or horsefly, is dispatched with a load of lead.

—27—

Theology and Pride

His Beatitude Conon, Archbishop of Bucharest, Metropolitan of Muntenia and Dobrogea, Locum tenens of the throne of Caesarea Cappadocia, and Patriarch of the Romanian Orthodox Church was slow to dress that morning. He needed to dress well since he was to be the Guest of Honor at the Baron of Meritei's estate. This, although far from Bucharest, was always a welcome trip for him. He would need to travel to the borders of his demesne, all the way to the Bucovina where many Germans, believers in the western Catholic church, lived. A small sneer escaped his mouth, "Catholics, what do they know of universal belief. Ever since the schism these so-called Catholics have claimed to be the true descendants of St. Peter and the Holy Roman Church. In their ignorance they still think they are the true successors of the church in Rome established by Christ."

He crossed himself and, interrupting his dressing, started to pray. Minutes later he moved away from the icon and finished his attire. After donning his miter, he regarded himself in the mirror. Not bad, the thought. I do look like a prince of the true church.

It was still early in the morning when he kissed his wife good-bye and climbed into his carriage. "I'll be gone for a least a week," he shouted to his wife as the carriage pulled away.

The road was not the best; the ironclad wheels of the peasant farmers' oxcarts had carved deep ruts that disturbed his reading. After a particularly deep rut, he let the book drop into his lap and leaned back into the cushions. The idea that the roads in Romania needed improvement to prepare for the new horseless carriages was on his mind. The world is changing, but not for the better. His thoughts continued to wander. People are drifting away from the true religion. At least under the Ottomans we had a common foe to fear. Now we don't even have that. Maybe it's fear that the people need to drive them into God's arms. Maybe these Catholics have it right with their paintings of the Last Judgment on the outside of their churches for all to see. That is what is driving their churches to thrive — fear of everlasting flames. He closed his eyes and allowed the rocking of the carriage to lull him into sleep.

That evening after a sumptuous meal of roast capon and suckling pig, he downed a bottle of good red wine mixed with sparkling water and heaved his bulk from the chair. The innkeeper hovered around him, anxious to attend to his every wish. "I hope your Holiness finds my humble inn and the bedroom to your satisfaction," he said.

"The meal was most excellent and I am sure that I shall sleep well in the room you provided. God bless you and good night." He made the sign of blessing over the innkeeper's head as the man dropped to his knees. "No, don't do that. It is something only the Catholics do," the archbishop said.

Two days later, the archbishop arrived at the estate of Baron von Meritei and was greeted in the most hospitable manner. A young boy of about five stood beside the baron. "This is my son, Alexandru," the baron said. "Alexandru, kiss his Holiness ring."

The Metropolitan extended his right hand bearing his ring of office. The boy leaned over and touched his lips to the ring.

""What a charming son you have," the archbishop said.

Alexandru ran into the orchard and plopped under a peach tree. For the last three days his father had never ceased to impress on him how important this visit of the archbishop was. "He is the most important person in this whole area. Even our emperor in Vienna, who is Catholic not Orthodox, speaks to him with respect. You must always be polite and always tell him the truth."

"Yes, Papa."

Alexandru wondered if this archbishop really was a holy man like those depicted in the icons. Has he ever been martyred, or is he going to be martyred? He thought. He looks just like any other man, only bigger. I like that crown that he wears. The jewels on it really sparkle. I wonder if that cross on top is really gold. I wonder what it feels like to be holy.

That evening Alexandru had to put on a new suit and wear an

ascot that constricted his neck. "Remember to eat slowly and politely," Papa said.

"Yes, Papa."

At the table the archbishop was already seated and when everyone else had taken place, he stood. Everyone else arose. The archbishop then blessed everyone and the food.

As the meal progressed, Alexandru paused over his food in wonder, at how much food the archbishop was able to eat. He almost forgot to use the right utensils until his older brother nudged him. The archbishop must have noticed his stare because he said, "Alexandru, my boy, come sit on my lap. I want to ask you a few questions. He waved at the boy, After getting a nod from his father; Alexandru got up and wandered over to his Holiness who pulled him onto his ample lap. "Tell me, Alexandru, how old are you."

"I am five, your Holiness."

"When is your birthday?"

"It is on St. George's day, your Holiness."

"Then why are you not called George?"

Alexandru looked over at his father. "My mother said she did not want a Georgi."

Alexandru's mother looked embarrassed.

The archbishop smiled. "How do you know that?"

"Mother told me herself."

"I see. Just because your name is George doesn't mean that you're a Georgi. You know what a Georgi is?"

"Yes, your Holiness. A Georgi is someone stupid."

The archbishop nodded his head. "Yes, it is one of those unfortunate and totally incorrect labels. But then, why don't you bear one of the names of your noble ancestors?"

Again Alexandru glance over at his father, who nodded. "I don't know, but I think it is because my brother Valerian is older than I am and is going to be the next Baron of Meritei." Alexandru said.

"I think you're right. Do you know what it means to be a baron?"

Alexandru's face beamed in a big smile. "Yes, It means you can have four horses pulling your carriage, not just two like everyone else. It means you're special."

The archbishop smiled. "Did you know that as an archbishop I am also allowed to have four horses?"

This was news to Alexandru and he stared at the archbishop with surprise. "No, really?"

"Yes, really. Not only that, but unlike a baron I am also permitted to have an outrider. What do you think of that?"

Alexandru thought for a bit. This was his chance to show the archbishop that he knew his bible stories. He sat up more erect on the Metropolitan's lap and said, "You can have four horses and an outrider. I think that's wonderful but, our blessed Lord Jesus Christ rode into Jerusalem on nothing more but the back of a donkey."

— 28 —

The Condom

I hesitated in front of the drug store. It had taken all my courage to come this far and now I had to go inside and actually buy one. This may seem strange today, but back then in 1962 you did not just buy a condom, you had to ask for one from the clerk. This is what I dreaded; the clerk was an older woman, but this was the only drug store open on a Saturday. How was I going to approach this old lady and ask for a condom? But I had to do it if I wanted to have sex with Gillian.

With trembling knees I approached the counter to face the kindly lady who must have been at least fifty years old. To her question, "Can I help you?" I stammered, "I want a condom."

Without blinking she said, "They come in packets of three or twenty."

"I'll take a packet of three.'

"Do you want Sheiks or Trojans?" she asked.

I didn't know there were different kinds and blurted, "What's the difference?"

"The Sheiks are a bit smaller and cheaper $1.25. The Trojans are slightly larger and cost more: $1.50."

She seemed to take delight in my embarrassment.

"I'll take the Trojans."

Once outside with the packet of Trojans in my pocket I felt manlier. I had done it; I had bought the condoms, not only one, but three and Trojans to boot. Now I could barely wait until the next evening when I would meet Gillian again. I would finally lose my virginity and, I believed, so would Gillian. The whole next day dragged by, but evening finally came and after supper I rushed outside and jumped into my 1943 Chevy. It started with a satisfying purr and I shifted through all three gears as I raced off to Rosedale to collect Gillian.

Her father looked at me with jaundiced eyes and stated, "Now, young man, take good care of my daughter and drive carefully."

"Yes Sir, I will," I said.

Once outside in the car I embraced Gillian and kissed her passionately.

"Not in front of my house," she said.

A little disappointed by her response I shifted into gear and headed south toward Bloor Street. "Let's go see, that movie, The Outlaw. It's playing at the Odeon," I said.

"What's it about?" she asked.

"Billy the Kid. There's supposed to be a very passionate scene with Jane Russell in it," I said. I was hoping the action in the movie would get her in the mood.

"Well, if it's a romance, let's go see it," she said

The movie was steamier than I thought it would be and Gillian let me fondle her breasts while we watched. It was very exciting. After the show I drove to the campus and parked in what I thought was a secluded area. This time when I kissed Gillian she responded with as much passion as I wanted. Her tongue probed my mouth and I eagerly took it between my lips and treated it like the delicious tidbit that it was. After a while my hand slipped down and pulled up her skirt so that I could reach inside her panties. When I reached her pussey I found it pleasantly moist.

By this time we were both breathing hard and I was completely erect, but Gillian still retained some sense. "Wait, do you have protection. I can't risk getting pregnant."

Proudly I said, "Like a good boy scout, I'm prepared," and pulled the package of Trojans out of my pocket.

Again she said, "Wait."

While I waited, not knowing what was the reason for the delay, she slipped off her panties.

"There, now I'm ready," she said.

I took out a condom and unrolled it over my stiff cock. "Now I'm also ready," I said.

It was more than a little awkward finding a comfortable position for Gillian, but we managed and I slipped into her.

With her mouth covering mine it was all I could do to keep

from thrusting as hard as I could. I was lost in the ecstasy when I felt her contractions and came in a gush. I was savoring the feel of still being inside her when she whispered, "A guard's coming." I pulled out and she slid over to her side and sat up.

I looked out her side of the car and sure enough, no more than two hundred yards away a uniformed guard was strolling toward us.

"There's no parking here," I whispered.

"Then, let's get out of here," she said.

I started the Chevy and we drove away, straight through the campus. As we passed the bookstore, I realized that I was still wearing the condom and my fly was open. I stopped the car, pulled off the condoms, opened the car door, and dropped the soggy rubber on the asphalt. After closing the door I zipped up my fly and we drove away.

The next day I was back in class on campus. After a boring lecture on Chaucer I headed for Hart House for lunch. On the way I passed the bookstore and there, on the tarmac in front of the bookstore, in the middle of the road, lay a used condom. The co-eds strolling past the bookstore gave the condom a wide berth, pretending not to have seen what made them detour. The men looked with curiosity, but I knew that I was the only one who knew where this condom had been and where it came from. I never felt more smug in my life.

— 29 —
Wojczek

It must have been in Innsbruck, Austria, around 1998 when I was there as a guest professor. My wife and I were staying in a lovely apartment, part of a onetime large farm in the middle of the city. It was called, *"Schmuckhof"* (Ornamental Manor House) and had been rented for us by one of my colleagues at the University of Innsbruck.

That's where I first met Wojczek and his wife. Our apartment had everything except Wi-Fi and TV. To watch TV we had to go to a large common room where a TV for general amusement was set up. We'd wandered into this room and found the only seats next to Wojczek and his spouse, who was busy knitting while watching.

"You are the Canadian professor?" he asked in slightly accented English. Our landlord — to increase the prestige of her establishment — had informed all the other tenants that she had a professor staying inside her Schmuckhof. In Europe a professor is a highly ranked personality.

I answered, "Yes, I am," and introduce my wife and myself.

He, in turn, introduced his wife and said, "I am so happy to meet you." The delight on his face was unmistakably genuine. We conversed while watching a game show. As the evening progressed, I realized that Wojczek was a clever conman. He regaled me with stories of his success. "You have to remember that all people are greedy. They will do anything if enough money is offered," he said.

I demurred. "I find that hard to believe."

"Let me illustrate with a story," he said. "It was right after the war. I'd managed to get a small cache of diamonds from a Jew that wanted to get to Sweden. I still had all these gems. I hope he is happy in Sweden; I was happy with the diamonds. At the time I was not yet married and eating in the restaurant of my hotel. Food was still scarce. A small wedding party came into the restaurant. The bride was not so young, but beautiful. After I had seen her, I bought drinks for the whole party. The bride came over to thank me. I found her most attractive and wanted to sleep with her. I offered her a diamond. Her eyes grew wide and she asked, 'For me?'

'Yes, if you sleep with me tonight.'

'But this is my wedding night.'

I pulled out another diamond. 'In that case you can have two diamonds,' I said.

She went over to her newly acquired husband and after a short conversation returned, 'Make that four diamonds,' she said.

I pulled out two more diamonds — the smallest of the lot — and added them to the other two. She giggled and grabbing my arm said, 'Let's go.'

I took her to my room and we made passionate love. So, what to you think of that?"

I looked at him with astonishment. "This really happened?"

"But of course. Now I have a question for you. I would like to immigrate to Canada. If all the people there are as ingenuous as you are, I shall have a good time. Will you help me?"

"Help you! How?"

"You can sponsor me. Coming from a professor, this will guarantee that I'll be accepted."

I laughed. "Now you are naïve. In Canada a professor is nothing special, unlike here in Europe. My word will not mean any more than that of a brick layer; maybe even less."

He looked disappointed. "Why don't we try?"

"What do you mean?"

"Let's call the Canadian embassy in Vienna and find out."

"Whoa! Hold your horses," I said. "I didn't say I would sponsor you. I'm not that naïve. Sponsorship would mean I am responsible for you and your wife's upkeep if you don't find a job. I will not commit myself to something like that."

He looked at me with what I assumed was surprise. " I meant we call the embassy to find out if your word has any weight, not for you to sponsor me."

The young woman — her voice sounded young — at the other end of the line in the Canadian Embassy in Vienna laughed at my request. "What made you think that a professor's voice carried more weight than anyone else's?" She asked.

I did not know how to answer, turned to Wojczek with a questioning look, and hung up. He gave me a sad smile. "You Canadians are not as naïve as I thought. At least your civil servants have a sense of humor."

— 30 —

Virginity

Andrea wasn't sure she liked Charley, but he was her brother's best friend and had offered to take her to the graduation ball when nobody else had asked her. So, she accepted. She had not expected him to do things in such a grand style. He arrived with a beautiful expensive corsage for her and with his father's big Cadillac freshly washed. Also, instead of his usual sloppy jeans he wore a most befitting suit that made him look like a young gentleman. She was sure this would be an exciting evening. She was right.

Charley was a most solicitous escort and an accomplished dancer. He did not crush her to his body to feel her breast squeezed up against his chest. They twirled and floated across the dance floor to Andrea's delighted view of envious looks cast by her fellow graduates. When the band stopped for a rest, Charley went to the refreshment table and returned with two paper cups of drinks. Andrea was grateful for the cooling beverage, but was a bit surprised by the unusual taste.

"What's in this?" she asked.

"I suppose that someone spiked the punch," Charley answered.

In her thirsty state, Andrea gulped the drink down and said, "Can you get me another?" She seemed oblivious to the effect the alcohol in the drink was having on her.

"Sure," Charley said as he took her cup and rushed away.

Three cups later Andrea felt like floating and pressed her body close to Charley's as they danced. He seemed to appreciate this added intimacy and let his right hand drift down her back until he was stroking Andrea's bottom. A warm, never-before-experienced feeling of warmth spread through the space between her legs. She sighed and nestled even more closely into his arms. He leaned down and gently nibbled at her neck. Andrea tipped up on her toes and tilted her head to make more of her neck available to his warm breath.

"Do you want to go outside to cool off a bit?" he asked

"Umm yes, that would be nice," she purred.

"Wait, I'll get us a couple of drinks."

"I'd like that," she said.

Outside the gym, the cool air was refreshing. Andrea sipped her drink and asked Charley, "Are you having a good time?"

"Yes, a very good time."

"Did you think that your best friend's sister, the virgin, could be so much fun?"

"I always wanted to go out with you, but never dared to ask. This is wonderful. Aren't you getting cold?"

"A bit."

"Why don't we sit in the car? I can turn on the heat."

"OK."

In the car, Charley turned on the heat and the radio. It was Frank Sinatra. She leaned against Charley and, when he leaned over and kissed her, she responded with a desire she did not know she had. She wanted to probe his mouth with her tongue and feel his tongue inside her mouth. Charley responded with a passion all his own. His left hand slipped inside her gown past her slip and brassiere to cup her breast. It felt wonderful to have his warm hand on her. She leaned closer to him. He withdrew his hand and reached under her dress to the place between her legs. Without thinking, she spread her legs apart and felt his fingers probing inside her panties.

As his hand caressed her pubic hair she sighed with the pleasure of a feeling she had never had before. Charley pulled her dress higher and eased himself into the space between her legs. She felt his body between her thighs and then there was a sharp pain as he thrust himself inside her.

"What are you doing?" she asked as the pain brought her back to reality.

"Making love to you," he gasped as he continued to thrust between her legs.

She wanted to tell him to stop, but the sensation was too good. She leaned back and closed her eyes. When she felt a gush of liquid enter her she pushed Charley away. "What if I get pregnant?" She was suddenly sober.

"I don't know. This really is your first time?"

"Yes."

"In that case we had better not go back to the dance. There may be some blood on your dress."

"Blood?"

"Yes, if this was your first time."

* * *

Fifteen years later, when Andrea again saw Charley, she'd been married to Gerry, another mutual classmate, for a dozen years. Charley too was married now and Andrea thought that his wife, Beverly, was very nice. They greeted and hugged each other formally. Gerry was happy to meet Andrea's brother's best friend. They seemed to have many interests in common: fishing and hunting, even though Gerry was a writer and Charley was a business executive that owned a fishing lodge in northern Ontario. "You should see the lake trout we pull out of that lake. Boy do they put up a fight, especially on a good fly rod, with a streamer fly," Charley said.

"I'd love to experience that, but a struggling writer like me can't afford such luxuries."

"Then why don't you come as my guest," Charley suggested.

"I'd love to."

"Oh, and bring Andrea. She and Beverly seem to get along very well."

"I'll ask her."

That summer, Charley's Cessna picked them up at the Island

airport and flew them north to a sparkling lake where Charley met them on the dock with four glasses and a cold bottle of Prosecco. "Welcome to God's Lake, my portion of paradise," he said as they stepped from the plane. "Beverly is busy preparing a small repast for us. In the meanwhile why don't we sit under those birch over there and enjoy a drink. She'll join us in a moment."

"What about our luggage?" Andrea asked.

"Don't worry about that, Joe will take it to your room."

The two weeks at Charley's fishing lodge were a dream. Andrea had never seen Gerry smile so much. He spent all day fishing and evening writing at a rate she had not seen before. His writer's block seemed to have been washed away by the cool waters of the lake where he swam after fishing. Charley too was a perfect host, but Andrea did not feel comfortable around Charley. Her graduation ball experience kept rearing its head and she felt guilty. On their wedding night Gerry had confessed that he was a virgin and she then lied saying that she also had never had sex before. When Gerry asked her in the morning if he'd hurt her, she responded, "No, I've been using tampons ever since my mother showed me how to insert them."

As they climbed aboard the Cessna, Charley said, "That was a lot of fun. We should do this every year."

"That would be great," Gerry replied.

As the plane lifted from the lake, Gerry leaned over to kiss Andrea. "That sure was a great holiday. I'm already looking forward to next year," he said.

"Yes, but we can't keep sponging off Charley and Beverly like that. We have nothing to offer them in return."

"Hey, they get our scintillating company. Isn't that good enough?" Gerry asked with a broad smile.

"No, it isn't. You can come again, but I won't. Besides, I don't enjoy fishing like you do."

* * *

The next two summers Gerry flew to God's Lake without Andrea.

Charley asked him why Andrea hadn't come.

"She says she doesn't like fishing."

"Neither does Beverly. There are other things to do: swimming, water skiing, sunbathing, I don't know. You'll have to ask Beverly.

Gerry didn't know how to answer. He also began to wonder why Andrea didn't want to see Charley and Beverly, but he didn't ask her. He accepted her explanation until one evening when he and Andrea were sitting across from each other reminiscing and he remarked, "Charley was your brother's best friend. He still is, isn't that so?"

"I suppose so," Andrea said with a rather hesitant voice.

"He's a really nice guy and we've known him since high school. Is there a reason you're avoiding him. You've never invited him and Beverly to our place. Is there a reason? We could invite them the next time we have your brother over."

"Well look at our house. Compared to the mansion they live in it's a shack."

"That's no excuse. They know that I'm not the best, or most successful writer in the world. They know what we can afford. Besides we'd invite them because we like their company, not because we want to compete with them."

"You may like their company. I don't."

Gerry sat up straight. He'd never heard Andrea's voice with that edge of sharpness. "What is it about their company that you don't like?"

Andrea stood up. "Look, it's enough that you spend the best two weeks of the summer with Charley fishing and drinking too much instead of with me. If you don't watch out you'll become an alcoholic like him."

"So, now Charley's an alcoholic."

"You didn't notice?"

"There's nothing to notice. Charley's just a good host."

"Have it your way, but I'm not going to God's Lake again. You can go if you want to, but without me."

Gerry began to wonder why Andrea, who usually loved to entertain, refused to invite Charley and Beverly. Well, she has her own reasons, he thought. Life continued like that. Gerry flew to God's Lake every summer without Andrea and became more intimate with Charley until they talked more freely about their lives.

One evening after numerous cocktails, Charley confessed, "I had a real crush on Andrea when we were in high school, but I never dated her until the grad party."

"Why not?"

"Well, she was my best friend's sister and all I wanted from a girl at that stage was pussy."

"Yeah, I understand. I went to the same high school and had the same urges. What about after high school, did you date her again?"

"No, I wanted to, but that didn't work out?"

"What happened?"

"She avoided me."

"Do you know why?"

Charley took another long drink from his scotch. "Yes, I think so. I got her drunk and seduced her at the grad ball."

Gerry was silent for a while. "You seduced her."

"Yes."

"That explains why she doesn't want to come to your chalet."

"Could be," Charley said. "You must not mention this to her. It seems to be a sore point with her."

"I guess it is."

When Gerry returned home he embraced Andrea without the usual enthusiasm of reaching for her rear and pressing her against him. When they let go of each other she asked, "So, how was the vacation, did you catch many fish and get a lot of writing done?"

"The fishing was good and I started a new novel."

"Oh, what's it about?"

"Later."

That evening when they climbed into bed, Andrea expected Gerry's overly eager approach to her after a two-week abstinence. Instead he stayed on his side of the bed with his arms under his head.

"What are you thinking about?" she asked.

"Virginity," he said.

"What about virginity," she asked.

"I was wondering why it's considered to be so important. What difference does it make?"

"None that I can think of. But it seems that men think it's very important."

Gerry sat up. "Not to me. It seemed very important to you when we got married. That's why I'm wondering."

"What makes you think it was important to me?" Andrea asked. There was a nervous tremor in her voice that she tried to hide.

"Well, if it wasn't important, why'd you lie to me?" Gerry asked.

Andrea heard the hurt in his voice. "What makes you think I lied?"

"Tampons don't break the hymen," Gerry said.

Andrea's hand flew to her mouth as she gasped, "Oh. " After she caught herself she asked, "What made you say that?"

"It's true isn't it?"

"I suppose it might be."

"Not it might be. It is true."

Andrea could feel the anger welling up in her. "Yes, suppose it's true. Why is that so important?" She asked.

Gerry's voice choked with sadness. "Because you lied to me. We started our marriage with a lie."

The tone of his voice pushed Andrea's anger from her mind and she felt remorse for the hurt she had caused her dear husband. "I'm sorry I lied to you. No, I wasn't a virgin when we got married, but since you were, I thought it was important to you. I'm sorry I lied."

"I'm also sorry you did. Your virginity was not important to me. What was important was that you loved and married me." He reached over to fondle Andrea's breasts. "I do love you and what happened before we were married, except between you and me, is not important."

As she felt the desire for her husband rise and lifted her hips to more easily move his hand to her groin, she whispered, "I love you."

"I love you too," he said.

— 31 —

World Shakers

I had not heard from him in more than thirty years and then I got this email, "Hi, remember me? We thought we were going to change the world." That was it. Of course I remembered him; we'd been neighbors in The Project, the graduate student housing, in Princeton. I even remember his arrival by taxi from New York. This extravagance shocked a lot of us. He and his wife were exhausted after their flight from Reykjavik and their little son was already asleep, dead to the world. They had made no provisions for furniture and together with fellow graduate students living in The Project we furnished them with air mattresses and sleeping bags for that first night. Yes, I surely remembered Sigurd Steinthorson, his wife Helga Lavransdottir, and their son Steinthor Sigurdson.

The last time that I saw them I had just landed a postdoctoral fellowship in Edmonton and they stayed with us for one night on their way to Yellowknife where he was going to pick up rock samples that were connected with his research. If they had not phoned ahead we would have missed them. We were living in this shack that was condemned a year later and when the four of them, oh yes, they now also had a little girl, Repna Sigurdsdottir, pulled up in their VW bus (after all, it was the sixties) and parked across the street from us, I went over to check. Sure enough, they were preparing to sleep in the VW bus and I convinced them that in spite of its ramshackle appearance we had room enough in our abode for them to spread their sleeping bags.

I remember vaguely hearing that he got a job at the University of Reykjavik in the Department of Volcanology. After that we lost touch and then just as I was about to retire this email comes. What could I answer? Yes, as fellow graduate students we had often sat out on our back porch till two in the morning waiting for our units to cool down so that we might get some sleep. Those units were barracks, built as temporary housing for soldiers returning after WW II to study under the GI Bill. As far as I know they are still being used in the twenty-first century and may continue to do so well into the twenty-second century. Anyway it was during these evenings that we shared our dreams of the future and of how we would make these earth-shaking discoveries.

So, what did I discover? Nothing earth shaking: there are other interesting subjects besides physics. I got to know people in areas other than physics. It is people that are stimulating and interesting, even more so than abstract ideas. It is some of the individuals and their ideas that I met along my life's journey that have proved, not earth shaking, but most interesting.

Take Al. He's a psychologist. He and I don't agree on what

life is about, but even when we disagree, I appreciate his views. They're right for him, not for me. The things he has done in his life: running away from home to Australia where he lived in a room above a brothel, working on a railroad gang in the wilds of Alberta, being part of the hippy scene of the late sixties, then going to university and graduate school to get a Ph.D. are more things than most people would dream of doing in several lifetimes. Al believes, or should I say professes to believe, that one should experience as many things as possible in one lifetime. He lives according to this principle, even when it endangers his life, although I must admit that he is also one of the most safety-conscious people I know. Still, how many of us would dare to fly from Edmonton to the Arctic Ocean in a homemade ultra light plane that we had built ourselves and that lacked many instruments? He did. His career also has been a succession of adventures. He was always looking for the new experience.

Then there's Wally. We first met when I went to the nurses' residence to pick up, for a date, the woman who is now my wife. Wally was there with Ivars, my future brother-in-law. In my excitement, I had locked the keys in the car. Ivars and Wally, like experienced thieves used a wire coat hanger to open the car and retrieve the keys. I did not meet Wally again until many years later at my nephew's wedding.

No great scientific truths, not even great insights. However, I learned a lot from my wife. Family is more important than the Nobel

Prize. Science will progress even without my feeble efforts. Spending time with my daughters, teaching them baseball and soccer as well as a love for literature is more rewarding than publishing another paper. The question I had to ask myself over and over again was, "What will have a bigger impact 100 years from now, a paper I publish or how I interact with my children and fellow humans?"

I also learned much from Ivars, my brother-in-law. I have this life and if I don't enjoy it to the fullest, I am cheating myself. Physics was my first love, before I even dated my wife. Physics is still a large part of what I enjoy. I love discovering a truth that nobody else knows. I am thrilled by finally understanding a complicated phenomenon, but there are other things I enjoy as well, some even more. If I dedicated myself entirely to physics, I would miss all these other activities that also demand time. Exploring life — how to live it to the fullest — is an adventure filled with wonder and unexpected rewards. These rewards are not the same as the insights from doing research, they have a flavor all their own.

No, I did not make any earth shaking discoveries in physics. At best, I inspired a few young minds. However, I have enjoyed every moment of my life and am satisfied that my daughters also know what life is about. My wife has been my constant inspiration and my greatest source of joy. What more can one ask for in this life?

Yes, years later when Icelandic Airlines had direct flights from Edmonton to Europe with a free (up to five days) stopover in Reykjavik, I again met Sigurdur. We were both retired. He had remarried since Helga had died a few years earlier. Both of us now had grey hair and he received my wife and me with great hospitality and besides treating us to a lunch at his house, chauffeured us around part of his country to proudly show us how electricity was harvested from the geothermal energy that both blessed and cursed this land.

Neither of us had become a world shaker, but we both had, up to this time, and continue to do so, led a useful productive life. Maybe one of our students will do what we failed to do — become a world shaker.

— 32 —

What If ?

It was around 1946, while we were still in grade three, when my best friend, Jack, left. One day he was here, the next day he didn't come out to play. We always played together, even in school. That's how we kept the other kids from making fun of us because we were so poor. Yesterday I'd seen him sitting in front of the building in front of that funny sign his mother had made. It was right behind him nailed to the door. As far as I could make out, it said,

BOY FOR SALE
INQUIRE INSIDE

Mom told me not to ask Mrs. O'Leary, Jack's mom, about him or the sign. She said that like us Mrs. O'Leary was having a tough time. Ever since the war ended and women were no longer needed to make stuff in the factories and Dad had not come back from the war and never would, things were bad. Mom had also lost her job. It wasn't until I was much older that I understood what had happened. That's when I also understood about all those men who came to spend time with Mom in the bedroom. She always made me leave the apartment to play outside before they came, even in winter.

I always wore clothes that Mom had patched, but I didn't feel poor except for when the other kids, yelled, "Sean's got patches, where every cootie hatches. He's always itching scratches." After a while, even though it hurt, I learned not to pay attention. Brother Benedict, the principal, would punish these boys whenever he heard them, but that didn't help.

Those boys made me know that I was poor. Mom was different. She always made sure we had enough to eat and once in a while we even had some meat — usually pigs knuckles or chicken necks. I even got presents on my birthday and from Santa at Christmas. When I go these present, Mom always hugged and kissed me and told me how much she loved me. I tried to get out of her embraces as quickly as possible. It was all too mushy for me. I'd have preferred bigger presents and less mush. That's why I envied the other boys that got really expensive gifts. I wished I had a rich mother or a father.

Eventually I finished high school and entered college. That's when I reconnected with Jack. I'd seen him a couple of times, but he always ignored me and I didn't want to intrude because he was a bunch of spiffy dudes. Unlike me, he wore new clothes that were right in style and belonged to a fraternity. I never did; I never got rushed, because there's no way I could afford the fraternity fees. It had taking all my savings from weekend and summer jobs, as well as a bursary and help from Mom, to be able to pay the tuition fees. Then I met him when he was alone and said, "Hi, Jack." He also remembered me and, after an initial hug, I soon realized that Jack had changed. He was sort of a king of the roost –– a real cock around which all the good-looking chicks flocked. He'd become what I wanted to be. When I asked him where he'd gone when he disappeared all those years ago, he got really angry. "That's none of your goddamn fucking business. Besides who're you to ask about that when your mother's a whore?"

Why did he say that? He'd never been mean to me before. I wanted to hit him, but held back. "What's so terrible about my question? And why're you calling my mother a whore?"

He tried to rush away as if he were ashamed to be seen with me. Before he left he turned and yelled, "Because that's what she is."

That's when I lost control and grabbed and slugged him. He looked really surprised when he started to pick himself off the ground. "You didn't know, did you?" he asked.

I reached out my hand to help him up. "I knew, but nobody's going to call my mother a whore, not even you. She did what she had to do to keep us going," I said

He took my hand. "So did my mother."

"What do you mean?" I asked

He looked at me with a look that said he didn't believe me and instead of rushing away asked, "You didn't know she sold me?"

I stared at him. Suddenly everything made sense: the sign, his disappearance, everything.

"No I didn't," I said.

He again gave me that disbelieving look. "Selling your kid is worse than selling your body to keep your kid and yourself fed. That's why I was so angry with you and called your mother a whore. My mother was worse than a whore; she sold her son — me."

"But, look at you, you look like you made out OK. You've got it all," I said.

"Yeah, I did fine, except I had no parents, no mother. The people that bought me, really rich people with a butler and all, only wanted a son to carry on their name. They adopted me, but didn't give a shit about me, and I now have their name. I'm now Jack Smythe, a real English name, no longer an Irish O'Leary."

"What's wrong with an Irish name?"

Jack again looked at me as if I were stupid. "Irish are known for their poverty and ignorance. They're mostly a bunch of ignorant papists. That's why they're discriminated against"

"You mean like the way me and you were?"

"Yeah, like you, but not the way I am."

This time I was shocked and my voice must have betrayed it when I asked, "You're not part of that Alpha, Beta, Gamma fraternity that call themselves, 'True Sons of the Empire,' are you?"

Jack stuck his chest out. "Yes, I am and proud to be so. We

represent the best of the English Empire."

"Do your frat brothers know that you were born a mackerel snapper, like me?"

Jack reddened and I realized I'd pushed him too far. "Don't answer," I said.

"Fuck you," he said and turned to leave.

I let him go, but I still wondered, "What if? What if my mother had sold me, and the people that bought Jack had bought me instead? Would I have become as intolerant of my people as he had?"

I needed to learn more. That's when I looked up Jack's adopted parents, the Smythes of Rosedale. I'd expected a prestigious house, but nothing like the mansion that was his home now. I could not imagine myself unhappy living in what was almost a castle. As I stood across the street and watched, a limousine stopped in front. An elegantly dressed man got out after the chauffeur opened the door for him. The man walked to the door and rang the bell. A man with the formal bearing of a military officer, probably their butler, opened the door, and took the proffered hat, and ushered the man into what looked like a spacious room. He was dressed better than anyone I knew — in a tuxedo of all things. Obviously the Smythes were a rather wealthy family and Jack had been more than fortunate to be adopted by them. So, why was he so angry?

Over the next few months on campus I ran into Jack again. If he was in the company of other men, he ignored my greetings.

But when he was alone he seemed genuinely glad to meet me. "I'm sorry about the other day, Sean. I just didn't want to introduce you to my frat brothers. They wouldn't understand."

I was angry the first time he said that and replied, "Understand what? That I'm a poor Irish Catholic?"

"Now don't be like that. I move in different circles now. That's all."

"You're saying you're ashamed to be seen with me."

"Not ashamed. But, being seen associating with someone like you would diminish my chances for getting ahead. Besides, my parents also would not understand."

"How do you think your real mom would feel if she heard you talk?"

"Fuck you! Can't you get past that? I have a real mom. Her name is Mrs. Elizabeth Smythe. She's made sure I always had what I needed. She's my real mom."

"Do you love her?" I asked.

Jack thought for a minute before answering. "I respect her."

"Yes, but do you love her?"

"She never hugged or kissed me the way my birth mother did. I really miss that."

"What about Mr. Smythe? Did he ever hug or kiss you?"

Jack looked on the verge of tears. "No, he didn't either. I wish one of them or both had. They didn't really want a son; they just wanted someone to carry on their name. They gave me anything I ever asked for, but no love. I just wish they'd hugged me once in a while instead of buying me more presents. The only one that ever hugged me was Mary, our maid."

I found it difficult to feel sorry for Jack. Yet, I began to realize that the meager presents that Mom made sure I got on my birthday and at Christmas meant more to me because of the way they were given than the lavish presents that Jack must have received. They must have cost my mom a lot more than Jack's presents cost his parents.

I never again pursued questions of the past with Jack. I now knew the answer to, "What if?"

— 33 —

The Train Trip

Central Station in Toronto was horribly congested as Professor Barlow pushed his way through the crowd. "Damn air traffic controller strike," he muttered to himself as he edged into the queue leading to the wicket. An older woman at the front was asking all sorts of unnecessary questions as far as he was concerned. Why didn't she just buy her ticket and get on with it. There were at least a dozen more people ahead of him and here was this old biddy holding up everybody. He noticed that he was drumming the fingers of his right hand against the suitcase when the tall thin man in front of him glared in an obvious fashion first at him and then, down at his hand. "I'm sorry," he mumbled. "All flights are down and I have to get back to Edmonton and I don't even know whether I can get a berth on this train."

"Berth," the thin man snorted. "You'll be lucky to get a seat."

He caught himself starting to drum again, just in time. The trip from Buffalo's airport to Malton, with the long holdup by

Canada Customs when they reached the border, had not improved his already vile mood. Everyone had to exit the bus to have their passports and luggage examined. As Barlow exited the bus he stepped into a large puddle of melted snow. The cold wetness penetrated through his shoes into his socks. He was furious at the unmitigated stupidity and practically shouted at the idiotic civil servants who had nothing better to do than to make a bad situation worse. The customs officer simply ignored him and continued to search even more slowly and meticulously through everyone's luggage. It had taken well over two hours for their bus to clear customs. By this time his feet were freezing. He'd hoped that the bus would be sealed and driven right through so that they would clear customs at Malton where they were equipped to handle crowds. But no, these stupid civil servants didn't have enough imagination for that. Customs had to be cleared at the border.

The line moved ahead, one by one, and after an endless interval, actually no more than twenty minutes, he arrived at the wicket to be confronted by a bored clerk who did not utter a word but simply stared past him. "I'd like a sleeper to Edmonton," Barlow said.

Without even glancing at him the clerk said, "None available."

"Well, what have you got to Edmonton?"

The clerk looked at him for the first time. "There are seats in coach."

"Alright, I'll take one. If a sleeper becomes available I can upgrade this ticket, right?"

"**If** one becomes available." The clerk pulled out a ticket, stamped it, and wrote something on it. "That's forty-two dollars."

Barlow placed two twenties and a five in the rotating money tray. The clerk placed the ticket and a one-dollar plus a two-dollar bill in the tray. Before he could rotate it back, Barlow said, "Can you give me two ones instead of that two-dollar bill?" The clerk's right eyebrow raised and lowered and without saying a word he replaced the reddish brown bill with two green singles, rotated the tray and stared past Barlow at some far point in the cavernous building. Barlow picked up his suitcase and eased past the crowd into the relative emptiness of the main hall. The big clock high up on the wall indicated a quarter to ten. He had three hours and fifteen minutes to kill before the train left. Time enough to go to the washroom and clean up from his overnight trip.

After a shave and his second cup of coffee, Barlow's grumpiness dissipated somewhat. He leaned back in the booth and stretched out his legs. All right, so he'd be three days late getting back home. So what? He'd phoned Kate and she knew what time to expect him. Besides a trip by train, by day-coach, across Canada in winter might be fun. Hell, he hadn't travelled by train across the country since the summer of fifty-six when he'd been in high school and gone out to Banff for a summer vacation. That was now thirteen years ago and it had never occurred to him then that he might wind up living out west. Yes, this might be something interesting, a new experience, seeing northern Ontario and the prairies pass by in winter.

Half an hour before departure time he boarded the train. The car was pleasantly warm and the conductor told him he could choose any seat he wanted. There were two young men and a young woman already in the car. As soon as he had stowed his suitcase in the luggage rack above his seat and hung up his overcoat, one of the men approached him and asked, "Do you play hearts?"

"Well, yes I do, but I haven't played for years."

"So how far are you going?"

"To Edmonton."

"Great, we're going to Vancouver. You'll have lots of time to learn how to play hearts again. We've got cards and we're going to get the conductor to put up a table for us."

Barlow chuckled mentally. Yes, this was going to be all right. Hell, it might even be a bit of relaxation, travelling across the country with nothing to worry about since everything was out of his hands anyway. Yes, playing hearts and looking out the window was going to be just fine.

A very elegant woman, in a full-length mink, escorted by a redcap carrying two matching leather suitcases, entered the car. All ten eyes watched as the redcap deposited her luggage on the rack and she handed him a two-dollar bill. She seemed oblivious of the staring eyes as she unbuttoned her coat and sat back in her seat. A few moments later the porter entered the car. His eyes also came to rest on the woman. With a small movement of a hand, encased in a kid-leather glove, she summoned him. As he approached, she reached into her purse withdrew a twenty dollar bill and whispered urgently to him. Without looking at the money, the porter took it, slipped it into his pocket, and hurried away. The ten eyes continued to stare. About ten minutes later the porter returned, reached up and took down the elegant woman's bags, and escorted her out of the car.

The same young man that had approached Barlow before sneered, "I guess there was one more couchette available."

"What do you mean?" Barlow couldn't believe that such injustice was possible. "I tried to get a sleeper more than three hours ago and was told that nothing was available."

"Yeah, did you offer twenty bucks?"

Barlow settled back into his seat ready to start seething again, but was distracted by a crowd filing into the car. A middle-aged man settled into the seat across from him, pulled a copy of the Toronto Star out of his briefcase and buried his face in it. Barlow looked around. Two women in their early thirties took possession of the seats behind the man. To Barlow it seemed that although they had tried to dress well, their clothes displayed that obvious stamp of the Army Navy Store or some equivalent establishment. Also their lipstick was far too bright to match their attire. He gave a mental shrug and looked further. A few seats down, across the aisle, with her shoulders drawn together and up, a girl of about fourteen or fifteen had just slipped off her shoes and curled her feet under her on the seat. Her short-sleeved wine-red sweater was obviously too small and emphasized the squareness of her shoulders and the outline of her adolescent breasts. Long brown hair with numerous tight curls framed her rather ordinary face. She looked frightened with her hands clutching each other in her lap.

Barlow gave her more than a cursory glance. Must be going to visit her folks for Christmas. God, but she looks fragile.

By the time the train started to move, the compartment was full, yet Barlow still had the whole bench to himself. Great, I'll be able to stretch out and sleep.

All the way out of Toronto, north to Sudbury Junction, Barlow played cards with the young men in the car. They had acquired a table and set it up. When Barlow finally decided to curl up on his bench to sleep, he noticed that the young girl had fallen asleep, huddled in the corner of her seat. She looked forlorn and more vulnerable than ever.

During the night, Barlow awoke several times, His feet were cold, but his head was hot. The heat in the car rose to the top and cold seeped in through the floor. In the morning Barlow was ready to curse the whole world. The toilet was occupied. He waited for what to him seemed an unreasonably long time before one of the women with excessive makeup exited. He rasped an unfriendly, "Good morning." The whole bathroom reeked of cheap perfume. He washed as best he could and dried himself with the paper towels.

As he strolled back through their car toward the club car, he noticed that the young girl was awake, but had not shifted her position. In the club car he ate his rather good breakfast and strolled back to his seat in the coach. On the way he again passed the girl. She had not shifted her position.

I wonder if she's eaten, he thought. He stopped and leaned over to her. "Have you hade breakfast. I did not see you in the dining car."

The girl leaned away from him and stammered. "No, I haven't."

"Would you like some breakfast?"

The girl stared at him with frightened eyes. "I don't have any money."

Barlow thought for a moment. She's all-alone. I can afford another breakfast. "Let me buy you breakfast." He said.

Again she stared at him with frightened eyes. After almost a minute she said, "Thank you."

"Let's go." Barlow headed in the direction of the dining car. The girl unwrapped herself from the seat and followed him. "Are you sure this is all right?" she asked.

"Why not?"

"I have nothing with which to repay you."

Barlow stopped and looked at the girl. "You don't need to repay me. I just want someone to talk to and not play anymore games of hearts."

They resumed their walk. In the dining car Barlow asked

her what she would like. "I've already eaten. I'll just have some more coffee," he said.

"I don't drink coffee. Could I have some milk?"

"Sure, but what do you want to eat? By the way, my name is James Barlow. I teach at the University of Alberta in Edmonton. What's your name?" He extended his hand across the table.

"My name is Rosemarie." She took his hand.

Barlow was surprised how, in spite of the heated car, her hand was icy. "So, Rosemarie, what would you like to eat?"

"Would bacon and eggs with potatoes be too much?" she asked

Barlow waved at the waiter. "One bacon and eggs with hash browns, one milk and one coffee.'

When the food arrived, Barlow watched her eat. Rosemarie ate delicately, slicing the bacon into individual small bite sized slices and taking tiny portions of egg and potatoes.

She's no ordinary waif. She must be starved, yet she eats so delicately, Barlow thought.

When she had finished eating, she placed the knife and fork beside each other and smiled at Barlow. "Thank you."

"You're welcome. Now tell me how someone with your good upbringing is all alone on a train headed west."

Rosemarie's smile vanished. "I'm on my way to Vancouver to see my father."

"Yes, but why are you traveling coach and without funds for a meal?"

Rosemarie stared down at the table for some time. With a determined gesture she pushed her hands against the table and rose. "I thank you Mr. James Barlow, but my travel arrangements are my private business."

Barlow also rose. "I'm sorry if I'm prying, but that's in the nature of my profession. I'm a professor and like all professors, I suffer from insatiable curiosity." While Rosemarie remained in a half-sitting position he continued, "I did not mean to pry." He hesitated for a moment. "Actually I did mean to pry. You are something of an enigma: a girl of obvious good family, yet seemingly abandoned."

Rosemarie sat. "I'm not abandoned, just on my own. I'm on my way to Vancouver to visit my father."

"Does he know that you're coming?"

"You ask a lot of questions."

"That's because I want to know."

Anger flashed in Rosemarie's eyes. "Fine! My parent's are divorced. My mother in Toronto has custody, but her boyfriend was becoming too familiar with me. So, I ran away to go see my dad. Now is your curiosity satisfied?"

Barlow leaned back. "Have you contacted your father? You should. Otherwise how will you get to him without money for a taxi?"

"I never thought of that. I just had to get away from Simon."

Barlow hesitated. If her story is true, she needs help. If

not, I'm a sucker. Oh, what the hell. "I don't know why I'm doing this, but I'll help you. We can have our meals together until Edmonton. Then, I'll give you enough money to keep you from starving until you reach Vancouver and enough for you to take a taxi to reach your father." He reached into his wallet, pulled out a business card and handed it to her. "This is my address, if you or your father ever want to get in touch with me."

On the way back to his seat with Rosemarie in tow he noticed two men in business suits nudge each other and whisper as he passed. He ignored their actions.

Two days later as they were nearing Edmonton, the two women who had been sitting a row behind him in the aisle across took turns using the washroom to comb their hair and apply fresh makeup. "We're going to meet our fiancés," one of them confessed to Barlow as he complimented her on her appearance as she strolled past.

Before disembarking, Barlow said, "Good bye," to Rosemarie.

Kate met him on the platform with a warm embrace and a loving kiss. "So, did anything exciting happen on the train?" she asked.

"Nothing exciting. I played hearts and met a young runaway whom I helped."

— 34 —

The Third Choice

"There is always a third choice." His words crash against my reality like surf against a breakwater. There is no diverting their force and I allow myself to be swept up in their foamy wrath. Yes, there has to be a third choice, not just the two they offered: a quick death from the axe or a slow painful death with all their fiendish devices and then the cross.

I stare at the dank walls where other hopeless souls have scratched their names and I struggle to memorize them. Yes, I have to memorize these names since that is all that is left of the lives they once labeled, of their hopes, and even of their loves. That is the saddest fact, not their deaths, but that not one person was there to sustain them with love. My death too is to be without love, only with fear and hate. They would push me with hate through that gate that leads only one way and they would not allow me the succor of love.

Lovingly, caressingly I read each name and send a silent message to the person who made those scratches on the wall. I watch the shadow rise from the bottom of my cell and, one by one with its darkness, obliterate the names. I know the exact spot at which the shadow will be extinguished as the sun sets beyond some obstruction outside my realm of existence. Outside my existence! Does it exist, this fancied obstruction or is this just one more torture, a kind of light show that my jailers play with me?

Why do they hate me so? Why is it wrong for me to believe in love rather than hate? Ah, my love, you were strong and I shall follow you. But I wish there were more love, less hate. What did you mean, "There is always a third choice"? At the time you also said that the world is not all black and white, not either right or wrong, that we must learn to see other possibilities. What possibilities?

The shadow reaches its designated point and the light on the wall above dims so that all is shadow. It does not matter. I know all their names and repeat them like a litany. But the surf keeps crashing, "A third choice," pause ... and again, "A third choice."

You were sitting on a hill telling us how no-one can really ever know what is in another person's mind, that we lead separate lives cut off from each other by our intellects and that the only thing that joins two souls and makes life bearable is love. That was the first time I saw you and heard you and I knew that your message was Truth. Love is the key. But what is the third choice?

You pointed out that since our intellects divide us, the choices offered to each of us appear the same, but they are not since what is "Yes" or "No" to one may be no such thing to another. Even the question, "Yes or no?" may be meaningless. So we must always be prepared for a, "Third choice." I understood you only partially then and I understand you not at all now. But before the dim light enters my cell again I must understand. I must! For otherwise I shall never understand and I shall have to make one of two impossible choices.

Are there only these two: betrayal and death by the axe, or death by the cross? Why two? Why only two? What if I refuse to accept their terms? Then they will choose the cross and I shall, in fact, have made the choice for them. But what if . . . ? No! That's not possible. It can't be that simple. Is that what you meant? Is that the third choice?

I sink to the ground and cross my legs to squat and face the wall on which dawn will signal its first dim approach. I now know how to make the third choice. I have a third choice and need only act.

I feel your love and that of all mankind. I am not unloved and alone. Slowly, as I concentrate on the wall, it changes. Its velvety blackness deepens to envelop me in a caressing love that I have only known in your presence. I feel the freedom of my soul and rise above this dust-laden body. Below is the town and yes, the wall that cast the shadow in my cell. There is the cross and beyond that the funeral pyre where some worn-out body is to be returned to the dust of this earth. There, far off on the horizon, where the dazzling sun is rising, is the hill where I first met you and heard Truth. I understand. I finally understand what it is to be human. I accept only one reality, mine, not theirs. I have taken the third choice.

— 35 —

Unexpected Family Connections

My uncle Valerian put his hand on my shoulder and said, "When I die, there are a lot of documents of interest to you. I have given instructions that they should be passed on to you."

At the time I was fourteen years old and did not care much about our family history. I'd heard that we were descendants from Austrian nobility, but how could that possibly matter here in Canada. We were typical immigrants as far as I was concerned: my father worked in a factory and my mother in a sweatshop. As my father said in his usual manner of quoting trite platitudes, "Grosse Titel, kleine Mittel," — "Big titles, small means."

I don't know how we lost track of my uncle or how he lost track of us. At any rate I never received these documents. Also I did not think much more about my ancestors except to mention on my website that my father was the youngest son of Baron Kapri. I'd established this site to try and publicize my writings. Thus, it was a big surprise when I received an email from Germany from Peter von Kapri, informing me that his daughter, studying at MIT had made the connection and we were related. We entered into an intense email correspondence, that still continues. He is a writer of stories depicting various aspects of life under the communists in Romania and throughout the world in diverse locales that he has visited.

Years after my father died I received another email from Paul Coman. Apparently, his father, Tiberiu Coman, and my father wrote each other often since Tiberiu Coman was married to my father's niece. I knew none of this until Paul Coman contacted me— again due to my website.

That's how I learned more of my family's history. Since I was now in my seventies and could see the end of my life looming in the future, I was eager to learn more of this history to pass on to my children and grandchildren.

There are two noble branches of the family. The Capdebo branch settled in Hungary in what became the region of Banat. The Capri branch — later in **1706** changed the name to Kapri, the more Germanic spelling — settled in Romania in the Bucovina. The family originated from Armenia whence they fled from the Mongols around 1239.

Now, I am trying to learn more about my family and have discovered — too late — that a descendant of the Capdebo family, Eva Maria Capdebo lived in Edmonton until her passing in 2010. I hope this essay will help me find more family connections.

— 36 —

The Proposition

The day of the party. Kate hopped out of bed to dress and get ready with all the preparations. She still needed to shop for some of the items for the dinner. The farmer's market on 95th Street was where she would find the freshest vegetables. That was the place she would hit first so that she would have the best choice before anyone else picked over the produce. Yes, that was it.

She slipped on her shorts and stopped momentarily to admire the fine shape of her legs. At 55 she still had the good legs and figure that had attracted Thomas before they married. A good thing too, she thought.

Breakfast of a piece of toast and coffee was all she allowed herself. I need to watch it if I'm to continue to look good. She lingered over her coffee, scanning the various headlines and toying with one of the puzzles in the Edmonton Journal. Enough of this, I'm wasting time; it's already eight o'clock. The market must be open by now.

She drove across the Low Level Bridge and turned right on Jasper Avenue. At the market she was surprised by all the empty parking stalls. Where is everybody? She parked the car and walked to the closed stalls. Closed. She glanced at her watch: 8:15.

How come nobody's here? I'll wait. They have to open soon. As she strolled back and forth in front of the stall, she saw a man stumbling across the lot toward her. Maybe he knows what time they open. As he got closer, she smiled at him. He smiled back and before she could ask him what time the market opened, he asked, "Hey, how about it?"

Momentarily, Kate was confused, but his appraisal of her figure left no doubt in her mind as to what he wanted. Also the reek of alcohol emanating from him told her that he was far from sober. She searched for an answer and said, "I'm sorry, it's been a tough night and I'm really tired." At the same time she allowed her shoulders to slump. The man again looked her over and said, "That's OK, lady. I understand."

— 37 —

The Big Tree

Just before you reached our garage stood this old, proud poplar. I mean that I was proud of this poplar, not that the poplar was proud. It was the biggest tree in the whole three acres that I owned. Every spring it was one of the first trees to leaf out. In the fall it was a magnificent gold. It was a tree to admire. But now it had to go and I would have to cut it down. I procrastinated and measured the area where my shelter for the boats, trailer and other equipment was to go. Even if there was room enough without taking this tree down. The tree was growing old and I had seen what happened to old poplars,; they rotted on the inside and a strong wind could snap them and drop them on a building. I could not rake that chance.

When I was at the cottage by myself — I did not want Skye, my wife to see this — I sharpened my chainsaw and approached the tree. It felt as if I were about to kill an old friend. I asked the tree for forgiveness before I started the chainsaw. To have good leverage to later pull the stump I decided to cut as far up the trunk as I could safely do.

The chainsaw bit into the wood with vengeance and I believed I could feel the tree's pain as it shuddered under the onslaught of the roaring saw. Eventually the saw chewed its way through the tree and it started to lean in the direction I wanted it to fall. After it fell I cut the tree into logs small enough to handle and moved them next to my woodshed where I would cut them into stove size pieces and split them to dry. The smaller branches I piled for burning in the winter in a giant blaze.

The next morning I approached the stump that needed to be pulled out of the ground. I had not counted on the stubbornness of this tree that I had killed. I knew that poplars do not have a taproot and using a pickaxe and shovel excavated around the still standing trunk That took all morning. I uncovered several very large roots. Trying to save the teeth on my chainsaw I set to with an ax to cut these roots. They were much tougher than I expected and by the time I had managed to sever the first large root from the trunk, my shoulders were aching.

At this point I felt it would be easier to re-sharpen the chain on my saw than to keep swinging an ax. But even the chainsaw had trouble with the hard roots and the soil covering the roots dulled the chain in no time at all. I continued by pressing hard on the saw to keep it biting into the root I was trying to sever. Instead of big chips all I got was a fine powdery sawdust and smoke. The chain was dull.

I again used the ax and chopped until my shoulders screamed, "Enough!" By then I agreed that it was enough for that day. Time to make supper and enjoy a well-deserved drink.

The next morning I set to again. By noon I thought I had cut all the exposed roots. After attaching a chain to the top of the log still sticking out o the ground and fastening it to the hitch on my truck I shifted into low four wheel drive and drove against the stump. My truck stopped as if I had hit a granite wall. I got out and examined the stump. It seemed not to have budged. It was as if the stump sported an evil gin, defying me. I entered the truck, backed up and accelerated forward. The front of the truck jumped up when I hit end of the chain. Again I went back to examine the stump.

Was it my imagination or was the gap where the saw had cut the root away from the truck a little wider? It had to be wider. I repeated the maneuver. Again the front of the truck lifted like a bucking bronco when I hit the end of the chain. This time when I examined the stump, I was sure that the gap was a bit larger still. Encouraged I repeated the bucking bronco action two more times before I looked again. This time not only was there a definite trench where previously there had been only a crack in the ground, but the remaining stump had a definite tilt. Also, the dirt had moved enough that I was able to spot another intact root. Again I used the ax and cut that root anchoring the stump to the ground.

After turning the truck so that it now face in the opposite direction I reattached the chain and gave another might jerk. The stump now tilted mightily in the opposite direction. However the bark had peeled from the stump and the chain had slipped off. I again turned the truck to face in the original direction and reattached the chain. To insure that it did no slip off, I hammered three spikes into the trunk. This time the stump pulled out of the ground leaving a sizable crater behind

As I stood there admiring my handiwork, I whispered an apology to the mighty tree I had killed. The spot where it stood looked barren.

— 38 —

Sledding Too Late

Fritz shot down the hill on my sled, down the steepest part; the wind whistled under the flaps of his cap past his ears.

On the climb up the hill his long shadow stretched in front of him. Most of his friends had already left for home. He slid down and started back up. The sun had disappeared. One more run, he wanted to do just one more run.

When he reached the top, it was dark; he was late. It would take thirty minutes to get home, but he'd ridden the big hill with the big boys from grade four and stayed as long as the oldest. He was too tired to run home. So, he'd be even later. Besides, he'd get heck anyway. What would Mom do?

The door to the house was locked. Why, what was wrong? He knocked.

Mom opened the door before Fritz finished. She looked angry. "What do you want?" she asked.

"To come in."

"You're too late." She slammed the door.

She was right; he knew she was right; he knew he'd get it, but not locked out and no supper. So, that was his punishment. He had to make the best of it. He looked around. The woodpile against the house might be a place to spend the night.

He piled wood to form a wall to keep out the wind that had started and lay down behind it. He was not yet settled when he heard Mom's voice. "Fritz, Fritz, where are you?"

Something was not right in her voice. Scared, head down, he plodded to the door, expecting a good thrashing. Mom rushed at him, grabbed him, hugged him to her and took him inside to a big warm supper.

Fritz wondered, "What happened?"

—39—
Saving

Right after the war, when all schools in Germany were still closed, my mother wanted to make sure that my sister and I would receive an education. The schools run by nuns in their orphanages were the only ones open. So, mother spent all her salary to send us to these schools. For my sister this meant that she had to go to the nunnery about four km from where my mother was working on a farm. For the first night I was also sent there until I could be transferred to the boys' orphanage in Augsburg, about one hundred km away.

I have never forgotten that night in the nunnery. I was seven years old and, as a boy, could not sleep in the dormitory with the girls. So, when it was time for bed, a nun took a candle and led me down a pitch-black never-ending tunnel. Every few meters curtains, like cloaks of evil wizards, loomed from both walls. The single light from the end of the hallway had faded into the distance and vanished when we stopped. The nun moved one of the shrouds and showed me into a cell with a bed, but no window.

She told me to get undressed and go to bed. After I crawled

under the cold sheets she left and took the candle with her, leaving me wrapped in murkiness.

At some point I awoke with a need to pee and groped all over the cold floor for a chamber pot. Nothing. Something touched my face — the drapery covering the door. I shoved past into thick blackness. Too scared to continue into this terrifying gloom, I pushed back into the cell's tarry darkness, groped across the clammy floor to the bed, dressed, crawled in and waited. I could not fall asleep again.

When, what seemed hours later I heard the shuffling steps of the nun approach, I waited and held my breath to make sure that's what it was. A faint glow crept from the crack beneath the curtain. It parted and the nun stood there with her candle. I dressed hurriedly because I had to pee in the worst way. The sister again led me down the interminable hallway. Finally I spotted a dim light ahead of us. When I told her I had to pee she moved a little faster.

I made it.

After breakfast they gave me large yellow pear to enjoy on my trip, because I had been such a "good little boy". One of the nuns had to go to Augsburg and would escort me on the train with her. I put the pear in my little tin box to save for later. It had been a long time since I had enjoyed a whole ripe pear all by myself. I wanted to keep the pear for as long as I could so that I could keep looking forward to the moment when I first bit into it and felt the grainy meat and the sweet juices dissolve in my mouth. I was not going to hurry this. I would keep the pear so that I could save it for the right moment.

I don't remember the train ride at all. Somehow, after we got to Augsburg, we wound up in this huge building where there were other nuns and lots of boys. I only remember that when it was time to sleep, I was led to a bed in a room filled with many beds. Every bed had a boy. I undressed and, after another look at the beautiful yellow pear, put my tin box with the pear under my bed.

In the morning, the first thing I did was to look under my bed. Yes, my tin box was there. I opened it. Empty. I closed and opened it again. Still empty. I started to cry. One of the boys in a bed next to me asked what was the matter. I blubbered, "My pear, it's gone".

Someone said, "Oh, that's Wilhelm. He steals everything."

Skai, my wife, also lived through the war in Latvia and Germany. Like most people in that region, at that time, she experienced hunger. She has told me about an incident when they were all very hungry. Each of them had a slice of bread. Her mother did not eat her slice but gave it to Skai and her brother to share. She has told me that even though the first piece of bread was as tasty as anything she had ever eaten, no piece of bread ever tasted so dry or was so hard to swallow as the second piece, in spite of the fact that her belly was still growling.

I also remember a piece of bread from the war. My mother, sister, and I were in this huge room with mattresses spread on the floor. There was a girl, whose mother had given her a piece of bread, with some rendered fat smeared on it. But what made this piece of bread particularly delicious was that the mother had also sprinkled some sugar over it. The girl was kneeling on their mattress, rocking from side to side with pleasure. I could not keep my eyes off that piece of bread. She saw me looking all the time while she kept rocking. Finally she broke off a tiny piece and gave it to me. It was every bit as good as I had expected.

When the war ended, the food shortages continued until one day, after my father had found us, he said that we had new money, the Deutschmark. Soon after that I saw and tasted my first orange. We had gone to a soccer game and I had fallen on the cinder track. Since I wore short pants, I had badly scraped my knees. My father then bought an orange for me; the first orange I had ever seen. The smell alone was something special, especially as I started to peel it. There was this oily juice that came out of the skin. It had an unbelievably wonderful smell that was totally new to me. My mouth watered as I tried to bite into the peel. My father stopped me and showed me how to separate the slices. The juicy sweetness was like nothing I had ever experienced. Yes, I gave half to my sister, so she also benefitted from my scraped knee.

Somehow, I think our childhood experiences have affected my wife and me in totally different ways. I no longer save things to enjoy later; I enjoy them now. I live life now. She, on the other hand, is a packrat. We have two freezers that must always be full of food. She has several closets full of material. True, she is an excellent seamstress, but she will never use up all the material she has accumulated unless she lives to be over one hundred years old. She is forever saving for the future, "Just in case something goes wrong".

— 40 —

There is More to Life

When I was still young and in high school I saw my future. I would be a great scientist and come home every evening to my beautiful wife. After dinner we would retire to the library and sit in deep leather chairs facing each other over a chessboard while listening to a Beethoven or Brahms symphony. There would be oriental rugs on the floor and a warm blaze in the fireplace. We would sip a deep amber liquid from cut crystal glasses. It would be a life of pure intellectual bliss highlighted by the passionate embrace of my ravishing wife. Of course I could never reveal this dream to any of my classmates who already viewed me somewhat askance since I was the "class brain".

The only girl that I dated on a somewhat regular basis was the other "class brain" and our fellow students found this most appropriate. Of course I also dated other girls whose obvious attributes were somewhat below rather than above the neck. Still, none of them ever really interested me. I was sure that the right girl would be my intellectual equal, although I never considered why such a girl would want to stay at home to keep house rather than pursue a career of her own.

My dream came true, but not in any way I could have dreamed. Brigitte was not one of the class brains, but she was smart and to my dismay, rather standoffish. I would have desired to ask her for a date, but her body language clearly said, "Don't bother to ask." Still she was a picture to admire and, even then, presented the woman that could fulfill my dreams . Her blue eyes looked at the world with trust and confidence from underneath gently arched, brownish blond eyebrows. A slight blush below the high cheekbones emphasized their classic shape of her Baltic origins while the hint of a smile accented the tiny dimples at the ends of her full lips. Heavy braids the color of ripe wheat streamed past her face and breasts.

So, how did it happen that she became my wife and more? According to her it started at one of the noon-hour sock hops. As usual, the girls were arranged in rows on one side of the gym and the boys on the other side. When the music started, boys would rush over to the other side to ask a girl to dance. On this particular day, Brigitte, my future wife, stood beside one of the class beauties, who had breasts much more well developed than any other girl. I wanted to dance with this well endowed girl to feel her pressed against my chest and set out across the gym. A classmate must have had the same idea, he rushed past me and arrived two steps ahead of me. I saw that I'd been beaten to the prize and, without as much as a pause, asked Brigitte for a dance. This must have impressed her no end, because she remembered this event, which defined me to her as a decent chap.

That was only the beginning. The second determining event

was the Engineering Freshman Dance, The senior engineering students had invited a busload of nurses from the local nursing school to the dance. At the dance I didn't know any of the girls, except Brigitte. I must also have been the only one she knew. We danced all evening and then I rode back to the nursing students residence in the bus with her. I didn't think much more about her. Actually, I did. I thought about how wonderful her conversation had been and how light she was on her feet. She was a cloud — light and responsive to my arms so that I only needed to breathe on her to direct her movements. After that I knew that I wanted to see her again. But how? Surely, this beautiful woman had only danced all evening with me because she didn't know anyone else. After the way she had acted in high school I could not believe that she actually had any interest in me.

Fortunately, I was wrong. Less than two months after the freshman dance she telephoned me and invited me to the Nurses' Ball. I was so ecstatic I never considered that her first, second, and even third choices must have already been occupied and declined. As I later found out, I was again wrong: I was her first choice.

After that dance I had the courage to ask her for a date and we started to go out on a more regular basis. Every time we met she intoxicated me with her joy for life, with the way she twirled and danced on the sidewalk as if it were made for her. With the way she saw beauty in everyday objects like a drop of rain on a leaf. The world was more wonderful and full of mystery with her in my life.

All this while my other all-encompassing passion was physics.

My youthful dream of being a great scientist had not diminished. Yes, Brigitte was important to me, but I did not think of marriage or any such possibility. I was going to graduate school to learn to be a great physicist. I had not calculated with Brigitte's superior intuition. She knew better than I what was important, or what I wanted. Life for me was proceeding as desired. I was dating the most desirable, exciting woman and I was well on my way to graduate school. Of course I did not realize that to become truly expert in my field, I would have to study under the top expert in that field. I intended to go from my undergraduate studies at the University of Toronto to graduate studies at the same school without realizing that this was not the optimum decision.

After we'd been dating for almost two years, Brigitte turned to me one evening and asked, "Do we have an understanding?"

For a moment I was floored. I was enjoying our relationship, but had not thought any further. She obviously had. I knew I wanted to spend the rest of my life with her, but I was also content to continue as we were. That's when I realized that she needed some form of security. I could no let this beautiful — in every sense of the word, not just physical — woman get away from me. "Yes, of course we have an understanding," I replied. And yes, in due course we got married and it was wonderful.

A few months after our wedding, Brigitte informed me that I was going to be a father. She was supporting us on her nurse's salary and I was still a student in my last year of Engineering. That's when I decided that I needed to find a job as soon as I graduated. At the time it seemed the end of my dream of becoming a great scientist, but It turned out to be the best thing that could happen to turn my youthful dream into reality.

I got two job offers based on my summer experiences and we moved to Wisconsin where I got to work in the Pioneering Research Laboratory of KC. This was most fortunate because there I was in the presence of two good senior physicists, an experimentalist and a theorist. It was a chance, although I did not realize it at the time, to expand my knowledge of physics.

However, after two years I realized that I did not want to spend the rest of my life in industry even though life was good and Brigitte and I with our little daughter were having the best time possible. The problem was that like all big corporations, KC was interested in solutions that worked.; not necessarily the best solutions, but ones that worked. I on the other hand wanted to pursue problems to their end, to find the best solution possible, not just one that worked. So I decided to go to graduate school and pursue an academic life.

In due course I was admitted to Princeton — something I did not even dream about when I was in high school. The atmosphere at Princeton was intoxicating while I was a student there: Eugene Wigner, a Nobel aureate, taught a course on relativity, Val Fitch and James Cronin who received the Nobel Prize for showing CP violation taught a course on particle physics. To top it off, Arthur Wightman, the world's foremost mathematical physicist, accepted me as a graduate student. It was glorious, especially when we were invited to Professor Wightman's home to celebrate the visit of another Nobel Prize winner. This is when I learned how truly wonderful Brigitte is.

It was the stereotypical physics party: the women sat around the periphery of the room while the men clustered in groups around the eminent physicists that were present. I attached myself to one of these clusters around the visiting Nobel Laureate. He was expounding at great length on some esoteric subject. I knew that what he said was profound because I understood almost nothing and also because he was uttering these words. After more than an hour when I was tiring of all this profundity I noticed to my delight that Brigitte had crowded in beside me. This was much better.

I placed my arm around Brigitte, who appeared to listen attentively until the eminent professor paused to take a breath. She then turned to face him and spoke in her native tongue, Latvian. The great man listened carefully until she stopped and then said, "I'm sorry, I didn't understand a word you said."

Brigitte smiled sweetly at him and said in English, "Oh, that's quite all right, I also didn't understand a word you said."

I dropped my arm from around her and I stalked away from Brigitte pretending I did not know her.

After that the conversation changed to more mundane matters, such as literature and movies. Soon thereafter several of the ladies rose from the edge of the room and joined the men.

Later that evening, as we prepared to leave, the eminent

professor's wife came up to Brigitte and grasping her hand said, "Thank you for what you did. These parties can be such a bore with the men talking shop and the women talking about such humdrum things as babies and diapers. Thank you, thank you."

On the way home, Brigitte seemed extraordinarily quiet. "Is everything all right?" I asked.

"No!"

"What's wrong?"

"You are. You're such a stuffed shirt, a real piss pot. Why'd you stalk away from me as if you didn't know me?"

I was going to hem and haw, but decided to tell the truth. "I didn't think that what you did was appropriate and did not want to be associated with your action."

She stopped abruptly and said, "Look at me. You knew what I was like when we got married. Are you ashamed of me?"

I shook my head. "No, as a matter of fact I'm very proud of you, but I wasn't at that moment when you spoke Latvian. What made you do that?"

"I got tired of you guys excluding us women from your company. That's not what a party is about. There's more to life than just physics. There are other interesting activities."

Brigitte had become rather excited and her eyes flashed under the streetlight. I embraced her and realized what a gem I had. "You're wonderful," I said. "I love you."

"I love you too. Just don't do that ever again. I expect your support ... always."

— 41 —
Schrödinger's Cat

Sagredo was alive — fifty percent alive if everything had gone well. So what if he was also fifty percent dead. He would finally be able to prove that he was right. Now, to write down the time and his reactions to provide proof. He'd planned this experiment for some time, ever since his last four papers were rejected. What was it the reviewers had said? "The Einstein-Podolsky-Rosen (EPR) paradox was resolved back in the 1930s and Schrödinger's Cat was laid to rest at the same time." Sagredo smiled to himself, "They must have thought they were very witty. Well, I'll show them witty, even if it kills me." He smiled again, "It probably will."

He noted the time: 10:05 and started typing on his laptop.

*Although most physicists today accept the rejection of the EPR paradox as well as the argument known as "Schrödinger's Cat", no experiment has ever been devised to test these ideas even though they strike at the **very** heart of the question, "Is quantum mechanics complete?" In this paper I not only present a re-analysis of these ideas, but experimental proof of their correctness. Since EPR paper will be vindicated by a proof of the Schrödinger's Cat experiment I* rely *on the latter since that is what I have put to an experimental test.*

I start with a short review. Schrödinger argued as follows to prove that quantum mechanics is incomplete. Place a cat in a sealed container with some radioactive material that has a fifty percent chance of decaying in an hour. Attach the counter to measure the radioactive decay to a device that will kill the cat if the counter fires. After an hour automatically disconnect the device. Then, according to Schrödinger, after that hour has passed the cat is both dead and alive; it is in a state of fifty-fifty mixture of alive and dead. Schrödinger argued that quantum mechanics asserts that, even if the device has fired, the cat is neither alive nor dead; it remains in a superposition of alive and dead until a measurement, say the opening of the container, is made. It is the opening of the container, even a day, or a week, later that causes the cat to be in a state of 100% alive or 100% dead. Observation forces a system from a superposition of states, such as alive and dead into a pure state such as 100% alive.

The standard reply presented to refute this argument is that quantum mechanics applies to microscopic systems and not to macroscopic systems such as the cat. Thus, when the detector fires, the cat, being a macroscopic object is dead and if the detector does not fire then by the same token the cat is alive. No mixed state. However, this argument has never been tested experimentally. I now describe an experiment to test this idea.

The problem with performing such an experiment is to know if the cat, if found dead, was still in a superposition of alive and dead prior to opening the container. Since any observation of the cat would immediately collapse its wavefunction to either dead or alive there seemed to be no way to test this directly. To exacerbate the difficulties, we have no knowledge of what such a superposition state of both dead and alive entails. I proposed to find out.

I constructed a large container, completely isolated from the outside with Schrödinger's fiendish device inside it. Rather than a cat, I placed myself inside the container and, to avoid being able to make an observation, which would either kill me or do nothing, I anesthetized myself to be unconscious until the hour had passed. This happened exactly three minutes ago. The device was turned on at 9:00 AM and off at exactly 10:00 AM. Now I am clearly in a state of superposition: 50% alive and 50% dead. As far as I can tell, I feel perfectly fine and am recording these notes so that when

*Salviati opens my container in about three hours and, I should happen to be found dead, it will be clear that it was the opening of the container that killed me. Should that be the case I would like this record published in the **Physical Review**. Of course my four previously rejected papers should also be resubmitted.*

Sagredo leaned back and re-read the manuscript. The laptop's clock would verify that he was able to record this well after the hour was up and the death device had been shut off. Yes, he would finally be vindicated. All he had to do now was wait.

Although he wanted to finish writing the paper, a growing sense of unease hampered his thinking. What if the radioactive material did not fire, but I'm still dead when they open the container? He now realized that quantum mechanics was more subtle than he first thought. The radioactive material did not have to decay and trigger the killing device for him to be fifty percent dead. No matter what had happened, if Schrödinger was right, he was already fifty percent dead. He didn't really want to die. Would he die when Salviati opened the container?

There was only one chance that was better than fifty-fifty: Schrödinger and EPR had to be wrong, quantum mechanics did not apply to macroscopic systems and the radioactive material had not fired. Much as he had wanted to prove that EPR were right, he now prayed that they were wrong. Life was too sweet to give up to prove that they were right. They had to be wrong and he was not only 50% alive; he was 100% alive.

* * * *

Salviati hurried over to Sagredo's house. There had been

something strange about his friend's note. "Come to my house at exactly one o'clock and bring your camcorder. Set it up to view the entrance to the large container in my living room so that it will record everything when you open it. Good bye dear friend." Why had Sagredo said, "good bye?" What was in the container?

As he opened the door, a large grey box, three meters square and one and a half meter high confronted him. He set up the camcorder as instructed and approached the door of the container with trepidation. The door fit tightly, but eventually he pulled it open. There, with an anxious expression, sat Sagredo. He rose and, stooping to avoid the low ceiling, came out of the box. Salviati grabbed his friend's hand and pulled him into an embrace. "What the hell is this all about?" he asked.

"I was trying to verify that Schrödinger was right about his cat and that quantum mechanics is incomplete," Sagredo answered almost sadly.

"Oh, sure, and I suppose you were playing the part of the cat?"

"I was, but since I'm alive I didn't prove anything?"

"What do you mean?" Salviati asked.

Sagredo explained the essence of his experiment while Salviati listened attentively. At the end he asked, "So, your experiment would only succeed if you were dead?"

"Yes, because otherwise how could I demonstrate that I was 50% alive until you opened the box? The only way to prove that

Schrödinger and EPR were right would have been for me to be dead. I'd have to repeat the experiment until that happens."

Salviati scratched his head, "I think that's pretty drastic, not to mention totally insane. You really are crazy if that's what you want to do. Let me see what you typed."

Sagredo retrieved the laptop and passed it Salviati, "There."

Salviati studied his friends writing for some time. "What time did you start the experiment?" he asked.

"It started at exactly nine o'clock, ended at ten o'clock and I woke up a few minutes after ten. Why?"

"Are you certain?"

Sagredo stared at his friend with an expression akin to anger. "Of course I'm certain."

Salviati smiled, "In that case you're one hell of a lucky idiot to be alive and not have wasted your life."

"What do you mean?"

Salviati pointed. "Look at the time at which this was typed."

Sagredo stared at the screen. The entries were dated today, but the time for the first entry was 9:58, not 10:07. He glanced up at the right hand corner of the screen to check the time on the computer. It read the same as his watch: 13:12. "That's not possible," he blurted as he turned back to his friend.

Salviati regarded his friend for some time before he answered. "You really are a lot luckier than smart. There are only two possibilities as I see it. One: you made a mistake and got the times all wrong. In that case you had no proof at all if you died. Or two: quantum mechanics is more subtle than anyone ever thought and the observation, namely my opening the door, not only collapsed your wavefunction to one of 100% alive, but the Time-Energy Uncertainty Principle was at work as well. The time's all wrong. The uncertainty principle didn't let you record with certainty your state, that is the energy of your body and the time when its energy changed. If that's the case, your experiment will never work and you and I might as well do something useful with our time like going to have a drink."

— 42 —

Retirement Speech

Today is the party. I'm going to have to stand up and say how wonderful it has been to work in this department for the past thirty-six years. How wonderful this department is. Wonderful!

What dreams, what incredible dreams I had back then when I first arrived. This department was growing in every sense of the word. It had the promise of becoming one of the best in Canada, in the world. I too had that promise. What happened to me? What happened to the department? Did I get too comfortable, too fat? How come neither of us ever realized our promise, our true potential?

That first year when I worked every weekend and every evening and when I was still full of the thrill of discovery for its own sake, not for the sake of promotion, what happened to it? What happened to me? Why did I change? I remember telling myself after that first year when nobody else ever came in to work on weekends that if I could not change the department, at least I could keep it from changing me. I still believed that hard work and a good example were enough. I had not yet realized that there was a power structure and that to effect change it was more important to become part of the power structure than simply setting an example. When did I start to become so cynical?

Get back to your speech. Stop feeling sorry for yourself. Tell it like it is. What have you got to lose now? Do this final gesture for the department. Reveal the truth. Tell your colleagues what went wrong, why we never fulfilled our promise. Tell them, that continuing the power system, the buddy system where hiring is done according to who is the best promoter of his candidate, according to who can make the best deal, is what destroyed the department. Show them how we missed hiring some of the really brilliant young people because we needed "an expert to bring in the research funds" and how we created a retirement home for worn out old hacks, who were still coasting on the work they had done ten years ago.

Well, what about yourself? Weren't you just riding on your old bandwagon following the band instead of leading it?

But that happened after I became cynical and disenchanted, after I saw that it was whom you sucked not what you did that mattered.

Really? Honestly? Or did you turn into precisely the sort of person that you despised when you first arrived here?

But I tried to get good young people hired. I tried to get the young Turks promoted. I spoke up against the power elite, the incompetents who kept hiring more mediocrities to match themselves. But they won every time. Every time they had a new argument how this particular old warhorse was going to raise the profile of the department, how he was going to be a leader for this or that particular group. Yet, somehow none of these leaders ever worked out whereas the few really young people we hired turned out to be real movers in spite of the fact that the senior professors, the so-called leaders, got most of the departmental funds and support.

As I walked out into the large hall and approached the microphone, I crumpled my prepared speech and stuffed it into my jacket pocket.

"Ladies and gentlemen, or should I say, 'Ladies and Fellow Scientists'? Today I leave with genuine regret this great and wonderful department to become an emeritus. I have seen this department grow into one of the best research departments in the country, nay, in the world. I am proud of having worked with so many outstanding people and of the small role I have played in the growth of this department. We may all be justifiably proud of our achievements. I do not want to list all that we have accomplished; there would not be any time left for us to toast each other. I therefore raise my glass and say, 'To the future of this department! May it continue to prosper and grow into the greatest department of physics in the world!" I stopped, and raised my glass. "I have spoken long enough. Let us drink."

AUTHOR

Anton Z. Capri was born in 1938 in Czernowitz, Romania (now Czernovtsy, Ukraine). He came to Canada in 1949. After St. Paul's School in Toronto he attended Jarvis Collegiate Institute and finished as valedictorian in 1957. He then entered the University of Toronto and graduated in 1961 with a B.A.Sc. in Engineering Physics. In 1960 he married Skaidrite (Sky) Kveps. After Anton got his degree, he accepted a position with Kimberley-Clark Corporation in their Pioneering Research Department in Neenah, Wisconsin.

In 1963 he entered Princeton University as a graduate student in physics and finished with a M.A in 1965 and Ph.D. under Professor Arthur S. Wightman in 1967. He then accepted a postdoctoral position at the University of Alberta. This turned into a visiting professorship in 1968 and into a tenure track position in

1969. Until his retirement as a full professor in 1998, Anton has remained at the University of Alberta. He also served as the director of the Theoretical Physics Institute of the University of Alberta.

He spent a year as an Alexander von Humboldt Senior Research Fellow at the Max Planck Institute für Physik und Astrophysik, in Munich, Germany and was frequently invited as guest professor or research scientist to the following institutions: University of Innsbruck, University of Pisa, University of Milan, University of Trento, Italy, University of Poona, India, Tata Institute of Fundamental Research, Bombay, Gifu University, Gifu, Japan.

During his academic career, Anton Capri published more than seventy research papers, five books on physics and chapters in several books on physics. In addition he has published six novels, a collection of short stories, and collection of poems. At present he continues his association with the University of Alberta as Professor Emeritus. He is also Adjunct Professor at Athabasca University, Alberta.

Anton Z. Capri has three daughters, one granddaughter, three grandsons, and two great grand daughters. He lives with his wife, Skaidrite, in Edmonton and travels frequently to his cottage north of Athabasca. His activities include writing, badminton, hunting, and fishing

Made in the USA
Charleston, SC
10 April 2016